Thank .

# Breaking
# Through

## A Stevenson Family Story

### L.E. Wagensveld

Breaking Down
Copyright © 2023 L.E. Wagensveld
All rights reserved.

ISBN: (ebook) 978-1-958136-39-3
(print) 978-1-958136-40-9

Inkspell Publishing
207 Moonglow Circle #101
Murrells Inlet, SC 29576

Edited By Audrey Bobek
Cover Art By Fantasia Frog

# DEDICATION

To my lover in the night time…

L.E. WAGENSVELD

# CHAPTER 1

As the oldest of three siblings, Sam Stevenson witnessed plenty of atrocities. On top of that, he had spent the last eleven years as a registered nurse in a busy downtown city hospital. It took a lot to fluster him.

At the moment, the churning in Sam's stomach had nothing to do with the gruesome evening unfolding before him. Nor was it hunger, though it had been at least six hours since he'd taken the time to eat. What sent the shock of nerves down his spine and threatened to cause complete gastrointestinal upheaval was the thought of Sawyer and Carmen's wedding rehearsal. It was happening right *at that moment*, and Sam was supposed to be in attendance. As eldest brother and best man, he was required to be in attendance. Sawyer had yet to lift the best man probation he placed on Sam for missing his bachelor party, and here Sam was, about to screw up once more.

Sam heaved a sigh, then instantly regretted the deep intake of breath when the onslaught of odours hit him full force. In the thick of summer, Sam stood in the hospital's Emergency Room. Everywhere he looked, there were lawn mower mishaps, cases of alcohol poisoning, and campers who had sought treatment for their various illnesses before showering. The plethora of scents was staggering.

"Stevenson!"

Sam winced at the crack of the doctor's voice and turned, holding his clipboard against his chest like a shield.

"Go on, get in there. It's not getting prettier the longer you stare. Surfer boy is next. I'm going to go out on a limb and say you should prepare for gastric lavage." She gave Sam a smile that was more a canine baring of teeth than a display of joviality. "Good luck."

"Thanks," Sam said dryly. "I'm on it." Drawing a shallow, guarded breath, Sam braced himself and waded into the room, ignoring the barrage of questions hurled at him from the people seated there.

One woman snatched at his sleeve. An angry rash covered the left side of her face and neck. "How much longer? I've been sitting here for two hours!"

"Hey! I got here long before you did, lady!" another voice cut in from a row behind her.

Sam forced a smile. "We are doing the best we can, ma'am. I am sure it won't be long now." He freed his sleeve from her clutches with a tug and strode toward the muscular lump sprawled across two seats.

As it turned out, Surfer boy was uninclined to wait for the stomach pump. The shift from lying across the plastic chairs to an upright position proved too much for his abused guts. The evidence of the man's excess squelched between Sam's toes with each step as he made his way to the next patient.

"Sammy, what the hell are you still doing here?" barked a sharp voice behind him.

Sam spun, narrowly missing a paramedic headed in the opposite direction. "Triage. My job, so on and so on."

"Weren't you supposed to be out of here two hours ago?" Sam's friend and fellow nurse Deena bustled down the hall toward him. With a squeak of white shoe leather, she nimbly dodged the same paramedic and advanced on Sam.

"I know, but—"

"Go!" Deena flapped her hands at him as though she were shooing a barnyard animal out of her garden. "It's your brother's wedding. Believe it or not, this place won't fall into a smoldering heap the second you leave the premises."

Relief flooded through Sam with enough potency that he ignored her sarcasm. "Deena! I could kiss you."

Deena came two steps closer before her features pinched tight in horror. She backed away, shaking her head. "Normally, that's an offer I couldn't refuse, but today, Stevenson, you smell like absolute shit."

"A gift from the other end of the digestive tract," Sam muttered. "You may be looking at a lot of overtime in the future, Deena, since my brother is going to kill me for being late tonight."

"Then get out of here! Seriously." She propped her fists on her generous hips and glowered at him. "I'm too old to work more than I already do."

Lacking the words to express his gratitude, Sam sidled up and sneaked a kiss onto her cheek before she could push him away. Then he broke into a run, headed straight for the elevator.

There was no time to shower. Sam snatched his wallet and keys from his locker, then paused, staring down at his feet. Muttering an oath, he sat and pulled off the wet shoes and socks, tossing the entire mess into the nearest trash can.

Barefoot, he sprinted down the hall to the parking level. Fumbling his keys out of his pocket, Sam glanced at his cell. Ten missed calls from his brother, five texts from his sister Sasha, each with more exclamation marks than the last, and two voicemails from his father. Sam threw the phone on to the dash without looking at any of them. He knew all too well what they were going to say, and nothing would save him now. All he could do was get to Willow Brook before one of his family members had a rage-induced aneurism.

\*\*\*

3

Every head in the room swiveled to stare as Sam pushed through a set of double doors and into the hotel's brightly lit dining room. His stomach clenched as tight as a fist, and sweat prickled across his brow. Doing his best to avoid eye contact, Sam strode to the front of the room, nodding and muttering a hello to any guest he recognized.

Like a criminal going to his execution, Sam stepped onto the elevated stage. The bridal party stared at him from behind their empty dinner plates and wine glasses with a chill in their eyes. To Sawyer's left, one chair sat ostentatiously in its emptiness. Guilt bloomed anew through Sam's chest. His little brother tracked Sam's approach from across the room, his blond brows contracting into a scowl so dark he could only have learned it from their father.

"I'm sorry. I know." Sam held his hands up as he shuffled to his seat. "There was a boating accident. Emergency was a shit sho—What?"

"Sam, are you all right?" Carmen, Sawyer's fiancée and the duo member least likely to murder him, craned her neck to see Sam around her bulky husband-to-be. Her green eyes creased with concern at the sight of his disheveled appearance.

"Yeah, I'm fine. Why?"

"There's blood on your face," Sawyer said, giving his brother a cursory glance as Sam settled into his chair. The steel in his tone indicated he was contemplating adding more.

"And you reek," Sam and Sawyer's cousin, Noah, added, inching his chair back as Sam drew near.

"I wanted to get here as soon as possible."

"A fact made obvious by your timely arrival and your unique style of dress." Sasha eyed Sam from down the long table. "Scrubs and sandals? Tres chic, brother dear."

When Sam frowned down the length of the table, she blew him a kiss.

"Deodorant takes like, what, ten seconds to apply?"

Noah wrinkled his nose, blue eyes twinkling. "Just saying." He was enjoying Sam's torture, the bastard.

"It's not me," Sam muttered, his face ready to combust. "Well, I mean it is, but some drunk jerk puked on my shoes. I took those off, at least."

"Hey, cut it out!"

Sam's heart kicked up a familiar tempo against the confines of his ribs. Charlotte Baker had been a part of the Stevenson clan for as long as most of them could remember. She had taken Carmen under her wing the moment Carmen arrived in town. Sam could feel Charlotte's familiar energy burning through his shirt as she came up behind him.

"You lot can screw off anytime. None of you spent your morning saving lives." Charlotte came from across the stage area and stopped, her hands on her hips. "I, for one, am glad you are here safe and sound, Sam."

Throwing her arms around his neck, Charlotte hugged him. Sam thought she sucked in a breath and held it before she descended. He didn't care. The sensation of her arms around him was too good.

To Sam's right, Noah was kind enough to look chastised before he mumbled an apology. Sam hardly heard him and didn't care, anyway. All that mattered was losing himself in the floral scent of Charlotte's hair. For a second, he allowed himself to lean into her body and soak in the unique radiance that was Charlotte.

"So, what did I miss?" Sam asked once Charlotte released him.

"Everything," Sawyer grumbled. He punched his older brother in the arm before granting him a reluctant half-smile. "You are going to shower before tomorrow, right?"

L.E. WAGENSVELD

# CHAPTER 2

"Ready?" Dan's thick fingers fumbled with the tie at Sawyer's throat. The knot he executed kinked to the side like an arthritic joint, and Dan dropped his hands to his sides with a grunt of frustration and glowered at the offending garment.

"Yes," Sawyer croaked. "I'm ready." His gaze darted from his father's face to Sam's and then wandered out the French doors framing the garden beyond. He stood, staring without another word.

When neither Sawyer nor Dan made any move to correct the tie, Sam stepped forward and nudged his father out of the way. Fingers accustomed to the delicate tasks of his profession made quick work of the knot. Sam sighed in relief when the silk lay straight and flat. Stepping back, Sam patted down the lapels of the navy-blue suit stretching across his brother's broad chest. He sensed Sawyer's gaze shift to his face but didn't meet his eyes. A sudden wave of pride threatened to close his throat.

The men stood in silence, breathing air thick with unvoiced thoughts and stifled emotions. With a bang, the door opened, and Cliff and Noah Stevenson rushed through, yanking the other three men from their wandering thoughts.

"Shit, Sawyer." Noah tripped to a stop at the sight of his cousin, causing his mountain of a father to barrel into him from behind. "You look so good that I think I might cry." He blinked his blue eyes a couple of times for effect.

A grin inched over Sawyer's face, and he shrugged, destroying the placement of his tie. Sam curled his toes inside his shoes and stifled a growl.

Cliff shared none of his brother Dan's qualms about expressing emotions and stared at his nephew with bright, wet eyes. "You got it right this time, my boy." He clasped Sawyer's shoulder and yanked him into a hug, mussing the suit jacket. "I knew it from the first time we met her. Even said to Noah that Sawyer met his match this time."

"Thanks, Uncle Cliff. I'm the luckiest guy ever." Sawyer's smile grew impossibly wide. "I'm glad you could make it." He pumped his uncle's hand up and down before reaching out to hug Noah.

"Wouldn't have missed it for the world." With a sniff, Cliff produced a tissue from his suit jacket sleeve and used it to mop his eyes. Dan crossed his arms over his chest and scowled at his brother.

Through the patio doors, strains of music quivered and took flight in the morning air, signaling it was time for the proceedings to start. Sawyer's complexion blanched at the sound. He turned and sought Sam's gaze, and Sam met it with an encouraging smile. "Come on, little brother, the rest of your life is waiting."

Sawyer squeezed his eyes closed, nodding. His throat strained at the top button of his stiff white shirt. When Sawyer held a hand out to him, Sam accepted it, allowing his brother to pull him into a hug. Releasing Sam, Sawyer extended a hand to his father. With a grunt, Dan grabbed his son in a rough embrace. When they separated, Sam fixed Sawyer's clothing once more and gave him a gentle shove toward the door.

Cliff and Dan slipped out to find their seats, leaving

Noah, Sam, and Sawyer to step through the French doors into the sunshine together.

\*\*\*

Alice had outdone herself, transforming the Stevensons' backyard into a wedding wonderland. Glass canning jars full of wildflowers lined the path to the handmade wooden arch at the end. Sawyer had meticulously carved the blue-veined wood into graceful flowers intertwined with Celtic knots. A nod to Carmen's Irish heritage and her wedding gift from Sawyer. Sam's gaze dashed over it, too nervous to appreciate his brother's beautiful handiwork at the moment. At last, his gaze came to rest on who he sought. Charlotte.

She flashed him a smile, her dark eyes shining. The late morning sun danced on her caramel skin and toyed with the dark curls gathered at her nape. Sam's heart clawed at his throat as he made his way to her side. He bent and brushed a kiss against her cheek. "You look beautiful, Chuck."

"Thank you. You clean up pretty damn well yourself, Stevenson."

At most weddings, the best man and maid of honour walked down the aisle as a pair. But, in a transparent move, Carmen placed Sam and Charlotte together and Noah and her older sister Marcy together instead. When Sam confronted her about the lineup, Carmen claimed she wanted to nurture the spark she sensed between his cousin and her sister. Sam knew his soon-to-be sister-in-law had killed two birds with one stone. If the woman didn't make it as a teacher, she could consider matchmaking as a career path.

Charlotte hugged Sam's arm against her body, hauling him back to the present. Together, they started down the walkway toward Sawyer and the pastor. When they moved to their appointed spots, the pastor raised a palm. All the chatter ceased, and the gathered families rose to their feet as one.

The music melted into a languid instrumental version of "The Time of My Life." At Sam's side, Sawyer made a gruff sound in his throat and rubbed the back of his hand across his mouth. Silence, punctuated by soft sighs and gasps, settled over the crowd as Carmen and her father appeared from around the side of the house.

Charlotte and Marcy sniffled across from Sam and Noah, accomplishing the feminine miracle of keeping their eye makeup intact despite their wet eyes. Sawyer lost his struggle for composure. Tears crested his eyes, and the force of his grin at the sight of Carmen pushed them to freedom.

Accustomed to distancing himself, Sam found he was not immune to the emotions swirling around the gathering like a cloud. The image of Carmen, her waist-length auburn hair loose and crowned in flowers, blurred in front of him. She wore a simple lace gown. It hugged her curves and complemented her height as it flowed around her. She put Sam in mind of the Fae queens of Tolkien as she floated down the aisle.

They paused at the arch, and her father passed Carmen's hand to Sawyer, joy shining in his life-worn eyes. The two men embraced, then the bride and groom merged into a private bubble of happiness.

# CHAPTER 3

"Hello, sir. May I join you?"

Sam swallowed before swiveling on his stool. "Hey, Chuck." Shifting his legs so she could slide onto the seat next to him, he brushed a hand over her shoulder in greeting. "Done with your bridesmaid duties?"

Charlotte grinned. "Nearly. I'm free to roam among the common masses until they do speeches."

"Ah, and you've chosen to grace me with your presence. I'm touched."

"You're wedding royalty as well. It's acceptable for us to mingle. Though I'm not sure how you escaped so much sooner than everyone else."

Sam shrugged. "The avoidance of people is a skill I perfected years ago." He tipped his glass to her with a wink. The alcohol had settled its smoky tendrils in his veins, relaxing his muscles. At this rate, he just might deliver his speech without vomiting.

Charlotte read his mood as well as she always had. "Don't get too comfortable. We are going up there soon."

"Lord, help me." Sam motioned to the bartender. "Another whiskey, please?"

Charlotte studied him, a mixture of pity and amusement

dancing in her dark eyes. She turned her smile on the bartender. "Two of them, please."

The bartender pushed the tumblers toward them. Charlotte passed one to Sam and clinked her rim against it.

"I can't believe Sawyer got married again." She turned to Sam; her eyes huge. "Twice to my none." She held up her pointer finger and thumb in the shape of a zero. "Remember how hammered we got at his first wedding?"

Sam took a sip of his drink. "No, I can honestly say I don't remember, and I'm at zero too, you know." He wrinkled his nose at her. "And I'm four years older than you."

He held up four fingers. Somehow, they had reverted to kindergarten counting. Carmen would be so proud. No, that wasn't true. She would roll her eyes and, for the hundredth time, tell him to retrieve his balls from wherever they were hiding and ask Charlotte out.

"I'm happy for them." Charlotte chased her statement with an impressive slug of whiskey.

"Me too. With only like a small side dish of jealousy. One of those tiny ramekins like they serve coleslaw in with fish and chips." He used his hands to illustrate the approximate size. Somewhere around the second whiskey, he'd become a hand talker.

"Side dishes. Food." Dimples popped in Charlotte's cheeks. "You're speaking my language now, Stevenson."

"Should I keep it up?" He leaned closer to her. "Cheeseburgers." He purred in a deep voice.

"Be still, my heart!" Charlotte pressed the back of her hand to her brow and pretended to swoon in her seat. Then she sat bolt upright and seized his forearm. "Do you think they have fish and chips here?"

"I doubt it." Sam laughed. "I think the dinner we had is the only one we are getting." The light played on the pink gloss coating Charlotte's lips, mesmerizing him. He watched them move for a few moments as she spoke, spilling words like magic spells, before using a swig of alcohol to burn away the ache in his chest. He should get away from her. Being drunk and lonely was never the state one should be in when spending time with their lifelong crush.

But Sam remained beside her, spinning the tumbler around in his fingers, caught up in Charlotte. She bubbled with laughter as she told him stories about work and the bachelorette party they'd held for Carmen. He longed to kiss her. The thought of it consumed him until he no longer heard what she was saying.

"Sam?"

"Sorry?"

"Will you dance with me?"

Holding Charlotte against his body sounded like nothing short of wondrous torture. Too late, Sam realized his head was bobbing up and down in a nod. "Yeah, sure. Of course." He stood as the song eased into the next. The melody bloomed, floating in gentle notes around them. Couples stood and paired off, making their way onto the dance floor. Sam faltered, and Charlotte's hand was warm on his arm. She felt him stop and looked up.

"What's wrong?"

"Should we wait? For a different song, I mean? Or until after the speeches?"

"No way!" Charlotte said, grinning up at him. "I love this song." She tightened her fingers on his forearm and hauled him toward an open space on the floor.

"What is it?"

Charlotte stretched up to encircle his neck with her arms. He put his hands on her hips, and his mouth went dry.

"What's what?" she asked.

Sam tried to follow as Charlotte swayed to the music. "This song," he clarified.

Charlotte blinked up at him. "Ed Sheeran, 'Tenerife Sea.' Only the perfect wedding song." She gestured sideways with her chin. Carmen and Sawyer were making their way over to dance. Some guests moved to the side, watching the newlyweds swirl across the floor, deep in a world of their own.

"Oh." Tears glittered in Charlotte's dark eyes. A soft smile curved the bow of her lips as she watched her friends dancing in each other's arms. "Aren't they the most beautiful thing you've ever seen?"

"The most," Sam whispered, never taking his eyes from her face.

Using the music as an excuse, Sam pulled her closer against him. The top of her head hovered around the middle of his chest.

"So." Swaying with the strains of the guitar, he closed his eyes, cherishing the sensation of her warmth against him. "Who's Ed Sheeran?"

"You're kidding me." Charlotte pulled back slightly to frown up at him. When she saw he wasn't, she shook her head. "Have you been living under a rock, Stevenson?"

Sam pretended to contemplate the question before answering. "Yes. A rather large, sedimentary one."

Charlotte wrinkled her nose but didn't win the battle against the grin creeping across her face. Night-dark pools that had trapped the glow of the chandeliers like stars. "Oh, you beautiful nerd, how do you have no life at all?"

"Hey." Sam feigned a pout. "I have a life."

"Your entire life can't revolve around your work, Sam. You need to do other things. Have other experiences."

"It doesn't." There was no conviction in the statement. Even he could hear that. Sam scowled. "I do stuff."

"Oh?" Charlotte's head tipped in the way it did when he challenged her. "Like what?"

"Stuff... stuff. I... read."

She shook her head. "And where is your date tonight?"

"Um, she cancelled. She's late. She's dead?"

The reluctant throaty sound of her chuckle rose above the music. "You and I both know that you never asked anyone to come, you idiot."

Sam moved them in a lazy circle, content to hold her and relish their banter. They'd spent hours like this when they were younger. Not dancing, but in each other's company, arguing playfully and laughing. "Why would I ask anyone else when I knew you'd be here?" Sam asked. Charlotte answered by laying her head against his chest.

Once they completed their rotation, Sam caught Carmen watching the two of them from across the dance floor. Carmen narrowed her eyes and pointed a meaningful finger at him. Sam grimaced. They didn't need to exchange words for Sam to know what she wanted.

Charlotte, missing her friend's gesture, dimpled up at him as the music eased away. As if she'd been reading his mind, she said, "I miss hanging out with you, Sam. You always make me laugh."

"You're the only person who's ever said that to me."

Moving her arms around his waist, Charlotte squeezed him in a tight hug. "Let's make sure we get together more. Please?"

"Anytime. I... I miss you, too." She was so close her perfume rose in the air and danced with the whiskey in his blood, assaulting his senses. His head tipped forward on its own accord. His eyes met hers, searching for permission, a sign—anything.

"Hey... everyone? Excuse me?" The microphone came to life with a shriek that made Sam's molars ache. Carmen's brother, Jake, jumped back from the speakers when every face in the room grimaced in unison and swivelled to look at him.

"Shit! Sorry." Jake's face reddened to a deeper shade than the man Sam performed the Heimlich on last week. "I shouldn't have said that. Umm."

How Carmen had roped her brother into being the master of ceremony for the wedding was beyond Sam. The poor man was worse in public than Sam was.

"Can the wedding party please join the bride and groom for speeches and toasts, please?" Jake shoved the mic back into its stand and dashed off the stage.

Clammy sweat pooled at the small of Sam's back. He

groaned aloud. Charlotte smiled and slid her hand through his and squeezed. "You've got this. Don't worry so much."

He was worried, though. Worried he'd puke or faint and ruin everything. Or do something else equally embarrassing that Sawyer would never allow him to live down. Swallowing, Sam let Charlotte drag him toward the stage. Guests waited in expectant silence; their faces tipped up to him. Sam made the mistake of allowing his gaze to stray to his mother as he walked to his parent's table. Alice caught his gaze, her eyes brimming with tears, and blew him a kiss.

"Sawyer—" His voice came out rough. He cleared his throat. The sound tore around the room with the help of the microphone. Unable to bear looking out at the groups of guests, Sam turned his body to face the head table.

"Little brother." Sam forced his mouth into a smile. "I thought long and hard about what words I would use to express what you mean to me. Then I realized you know me well enough to understand my being up here is the real testament of love." Sam drew a deep breath and adjusted the mic, hoping no one would notice the way his hands trembled. "You're an asshole, by the way. Noah would have been better at this."

A smattering of laughter rang around the room. Noah saluted him from his seat beside Marcy.

"The only thing I need you to know and understand is how proud of you I am. There were times, watching you grow up, I thought, 'this kid is insane.' You were the one who did the things I could never do. You jumped off bridges and raced your bike the fastest. You never let fear stop you." Sam paused, forcing back the thickness in his throat.

"You hurt yourself so many damn times, Sawyer, that it was because of you I went into medicine. I called Dad at the shop all those times to say, 'Sawyer twisted his ankle again. Don't worry, I wrapped it up and iced it. Mom says to pick up milk on the way home.' It became second nature, the natural next step."

Sam glanced down at his parents despite his promise to himself not to. He could not place the expression on his father's granite features, but beside him, Alice clung to her husband's arm, tears running over her cheeks unchecked. Sam's vision blurred, and he turned his gaze back to his brother.

"There were so many times I wished you'd slow down. I worried about you. Probably more than a normal kid should worry, but I wasn't any better at being normal back then than I am now." A few more laughs crackled around the room.

"Then you met Carmen, and for the first time in our lives, I saw you get scared of something. Not of her or the love growing between you, but of what would happen if you lost her. Some of us would have let the fear paralyze us." Sam glanced through his lashes at where Charlotte stood to the side, dabbing her eyes. "You didn't. You knew better than to let her go; you fought. For that, I admire you. Hell, I envy you." He laughed wryly, then winced. That wasn't on the sweaty cue cards he clutched in his hand.

"Carmen, I will not stand here and tell you to treat my brother right or to make him happy. You've already perfected those feats, and I'm sure it wasn't easy." He met Carmen's smile with his own and winked. "You are the most genuine and giving person. I couldn't be happier to call you my sister. Welcome to our crazy family. Are you sure you know what you're getting into?" Sam grinned at the pair of them and picked up his beer from the podium, raising it. "To Sawyer and Carmen!"

An echoing cheer went up. Sawyer and Carmen descended, sweeping him into a tearful group hug. "Thank you, Sam." Sawyer scrubbed a hand over his face. "Damn it. This wedding has turned me into a crybaby. Dad is probably so ashamed." Then he laughed and grabbed Sam in another hug.

"You're welcome." Sam freed himself from his brother

and bent over to kiss Carmen's cheek. "Every word is true. I love you both." Their grinning face swam in front of him. "For frig sake," he said, "have some babies already so Mom will get off my back."

***

"So, we've established my date is non-existent, but where's yours?" Sam met Charlotte's eyes over the rim of his glass as he drank. The two reconvened at the bar as soon as the speeches ended, and they had filled their obligatory hug quotas. The bartender slid tumblers toward them as they sat down without being asked. Sam tipped him ten bucks with a grateful nod of his head.

Charlotte shrugged a shoulder. "Cancelled last minute. It wasn't a big deal. I was so busy I panicked and asked a guy who comes into the café."

She took a long sip from the glass she cradled between her hands. The fumes from his drink tickled Sam's nose, and some of the stress released him from its hold. The hard part was over. Now they could drink together, laugh, and enjoy the rest of the evening.

Sam continued to watch Charlotte. She drained her glass and signaled the bartender for another round, this time ordering a glass of merlot. Vague unease shadowed her eyes, betrayed by the way her hands fidgeted with the hem of her dress.

"You know what pisses me off the most?" she blurted. "I've been up since four AM. I haven't eaten bread in months, so I could fit my dress, and the bastards messed up the sizes, anyway." She held her arms out to the side. The peach lace across her breasts sagged when she breathed out. Sam's gaze drifted down, then jerked back to her face. She didn't seem to notice the blush that he knew was creeping over his face.

"I could have been scarfing carbs this whole time, Sam! Instead, I've been suffering in a breadless world for three weeks."

Sam laughed, watching her over the rim of his glass. "I thought you said a month?"

She wrinkled her nose. "Okay, it was two weeks... It was one week, okay! One week without bread!" Charlotte hissed, her eyes going huge.

"That's the saddest story I've ever heard." Sam struggled to hold back a smile. Extending his hand, he rubbed his knuckles across the silky skin of her arm in condolence.

"Damn Sam, always so nice." She wrinkled her nose at him and giggled. "Damn Sam. I should start calling you that in revenge for the whole Chuck debacle."

"Hey now, that was all Sawyer. I had nothing to do with it."

"You could have stopped him!" There was no heat in her words, but she slapped his knee with the back of her hand.

"It was funny. Calling the cute, short girl Chuck is what passes as irony to teenage boys."

She cocked her head, studying him. "You thought I was cute?"

Sam snorted. "Of course, I did. You were cute, so sassy, with your crazy pile of curls all piled on top of your head."

"Do you still think I'm cute?" Blood tinted her cheeks as soon as the words were out, but she held his gaze.

"No." Sam shook his head, biting his lip to keep his grin in check.

"Oh." She tore her eyes away, burying her face in her glass.

"Now," he said, leaning in close enough that he could feel the warmth of her seep into his skin, "I think you're beautiful."

Charlotte inhaled the swallow of wine she'd taken. "Oh?" she spluttered, blinking at him. "Thank you." She brushed her fingers against the bare skin of his forearm. Goosebumps rose traitorously in response, and he suppressed a shiver. Sam turned his hand, tangling his fingers with hers and holding on.

"Sam." Charlotte stared down at their joined hands, then into his face, her eyes searching.

"Chuck." He countered, giving her hand a gentle tug. She leaned the barest inch toward him. Sam's heart threatened to pound from between his ribs. He wasn't sure what he had started, but his body hummed with adrenaline and excitement.

"Sam?" Charlotte repeated.

Sam raised his free hand and brushed a strand of hair off her cheek. Her tongue flicked out to dab her wine-stained lips. A burning ache squeezed his chest; years of wanting, exacerbated by loneliness and alcohol, by the romance palpable in the air. "The Time of My Life" came on over the speakers. It was the third time the DJ played it after spouting nonsense about Sawyer's favourite song. Carmen burst into laughter every time it came on.

Around them, people moved to the dance floor. Charlotte's gaze darted off after them wistfully, then returned to his. The two of them remained at the bar, entangled within the moment they had created.

Charlotte was nervous. Excited. Both. Her lips parted, and the lace dress fluttered at her chest, sped by the increased rhythm of her breathing. Sam noted the signs out of habit, so accustomed to monitoring the human body's reactions, he did it subconsciously.

Sam loosened one finger and stroked the pad over the silk skin of her wrist. Lifting her hand, he pressed his lips to the blue ribbon pulsing there.

A shuddery breath escaped Charlotte. She tipped closer until her knees pressed against the insides of his. It was a rush to touch her. Everything he'd hoped for and imagined. The sensation set his head spinning.

Sam lowered his fingers, skimming them behind her knee to the whisper-thin skin there. Charlotte shivered. Sam tightened his grip, pulling her to the edge of the stool with a firm tug. The scents of wine and rose perfume teased him.

Something base and primal beneath the notes encouraged him. Unsure of when he last inhaled, Sam, drew a ragged breath and raised his other hand, sliding it up her neck to cup her jaw. Her pulse beat frantically beneath her skin.

Sam leaned forward and brushed his mouth against the bow of her upper lip. Her breath left her in a shudder, but she didn't pull away. Sam's pulse beat like a snare drum. He kissed her. Kissed her the way he dreamed of for so long— years of kisses in one. He pulled the full pout of her bottom lip between his and tasted the richness of the wine lingering there. Pushing his fingers into the cluster of curls at the base of her neck, Sam tipped her head back, delving deeper into her mouth.

"Sam—" Charlotte broke away, pushing his chest with trembling hands. Reality rushed back like a slap in the face. Sam stared down at her, breath surging through his lungs in raging gasps. He was on his feet, towering over her. When had he stood?

"I... I—" Should he apologize? He shoved his hands into his hair and took a step back from her. How did someone apologize for doing something they longed for, something they didn't regret?

Charlotte stared up at him, eyes heavy-lidded before her gaze fell to their joined hands. "Can we go to your room?" she whispered. Every drop of moisture in Sam's mouth evaporated.

"Hell yes. I mean, yes, of course." He glanced around. If anyone had been paying attention to them, they weren't any longer. Sam knew only a minute had passed while they kissed, even if it seemed a lifetime to him. Hands still twined, he drew Charlotte to her feet, patting his pocket to ensure the key card for his room was inside.

L.E. WAGENSVELD

# CHAPTER 4

Sam pushed the door open and guided Charlotte through with a hand on the small of her back. "You're not sharing with anyone?" she asked, dropping her handbag onto a chair and glancing around.

"Noah, but he can figure something else out. Karma for his remarks yesterday on my smell." He flashed her a grin and pushed the door shut behind him with his foot. "The way he and Marcy were getting on, it shouldn't be much of a problem. In fact, I bet we are doing him a favor."

Charlotte laughed, bending to slip the sandals off her feet. Sam stood frozen at the door, studying her. Isolated from booze and the intoxicating vibes of wedding romance, his courage waned. "Chuck, I—"

She didn't allow him to finish. His back slammed into the door as her body crashed into him. Sam's hands came up and caught her by the hips. Her arms encircled his neck, and she pulled his mouth down to meet hers. With the vigor she displayed in everything she did, Charlotte kissed him. Her tongue tagged his, sweet with the flavours of wine and peach lips gloss.

Charlotte's round hips pressed against his. The muscles strained beneath his palms as she pushed onto her toes. A whimper vibrated in his mouth. Who it originated from, Sam wasn't sure.

She pulled back, her lips swollen, her neck and cheeks mottled from the rub of his five o'clock shadow. "Where's the condom?"

Sam stared at her for a moment, head swimming. "Condom?"

"Yes. You know, little rubber thing? Saves people from the consequences of their drunken nights much like this one?" Her dark eyes sparkled.

Sam let his head thud against the door. "Shit," he mumbled.

"Shit?"

"How do I not have a condom?" he growled, allowing his head to flop against the door with a dull *thud*.

"God, Sam," Charlotte groaned, pressing her forehead to his. "Are you serious? I thought guys packed them in their wallets from the time their balls dropped. Like the condom of hope? And it sits there so long it wears a ring shape in the leather!"

A powerful urge to cry with frustration strangled him. Attempting to battle enough blood back into place to form a plan, he shoved the hair off his brow. Charlotte thwarted his efforts to regain composure by using his tie to pull his face to her level and kissing him.

"Go. Find. One." She growled in his mouth. "There was a basket of toiletries in the ladies' room. There were a few in there. Let's hope all the horny people in this place haven't used them up."

"Okay." Sam nodded vigorously. "Okay, I can do that."

"Go!" She smacked his ass as Sam turned and rushed out of the room.

One left, hidden under a stack of tampons. Sam resisted the urge to kiss the tin foil packet as he rushed out of the washroom.

"Sam? What the hell?"

In his haste, he nearly barreled over Carmen's sister as

she came around the corner. "Marcy. Hey—"

Her pale brows arched, and she cocked her head at him. "What were you doing in the ladies' room?"

Sam looked at her, opened his mouth. Then snapped it closed again, unable to make himself care about politeness at the moment.

"Sorry, gotta go." He slipped past her and ran down the hall. As he rushed back toward the elevator, a disgruntled "Shit!" echoed from the washroom.

"Chuck?" The room was silent as Sam eased the deadbolt into place with a click and turned. Charlotte lay curled up in the middle of one of the queen-sized beds.

"Are you awake?" He already knew the answer, but he had to try. His body wouldn't have it any other way. With a sigh that slumped his entire body, Sam padded over to the other bed and pulled the comforter off. After covering Chuck with the quilt, he went into the washroom and cranked the shower to full blast.

***

"Good morning, sleepyhead," Carmen said when Sam entered the hotel's dining room the following morning. Sawyer sat at her side, his head propped on his hand while he methodically shoved toast into his mouth. He looked as exhausted as Sam felt, but for presumably much more satisfying reasons. At Sam's sigh, Sawyer cocked his head at his brother. There was a low hum of chatter from other guests, but they were some of the first to face the day.

"I wish I were a sleepyhead," Sam said, slumping into a chair beside Carmen. "I'm not sure I slept a single wink."

"Intriguing," Sawyer said, shoving a piece of bacon into his mouth and chewing as he stared Sam down.

"Stop it, you're freaking me out." Sam dragged the coffee carafe in front of him and then stared longingly at the cream until Carmen sighed and passed it over to him. Sam groaned in response and sloshed a healthy dollop into his cup.

"You didn't go to bed alone last night, so don't even bother trying to distract me," Sawyer said, seizing his coffee cup. Being presented with Sam's discomfort and the foulness of his mood seemed to have invigorated Sawyer. He was eating like a starving man, and it only drove the sliver of frustration further into Sam's heart. He glared across the table at his brother.

"Why would you think that?" he asked, turning his attention to his mug rather than face his brother.

"Because we ran into Noah sitting in the hall outside your door, flicking the *Do Not Disturb* sign and lamenting the fact he had nowhere to sleep."

Sam winced. In the excitement of having Charlotte in his arms and his room, he'd forgotten about his cousin.

Carmen released a funny little squeak of excitement and put her mug down with a grin. "Don't worry, Sammy, Noah found somewhere to sleep." The look on her face told him she was about to burst at the seams if he didn't hurry and ask where. He blinked at her once, slowly, because he was her brother now and had to torture her a little, then asked. "Where did he find a place to sleep, Carm?"

"In Marcy's room!" Carmen announced in a voice that should have been a whisper but hadn't known its strength. She clasped both hands over her mouth, then leaned closer to him. "Sawyer went out to get us more ice, and he saw him going inside."

Carmen's older sister, Marcy, had planned to bring her twin sons to the wedding. At the last minute, their grandparents on their father's side asked if the boys could stay with them for the weekend. Sam sensed it wasn't a straightforward decision for Marcy—he knew a bit about the family's tumultuous history from Sawyer—but in the end, she left the boys and drove up alone. Sam shrugged. "Maybe your sister took pity on him and let him use the extra bed the twins were going to sleep in."

Carmen's red-brown brows drew together. "No, Sam

26

Stevenson. They made love all night, and now they can't live without each other. They are going to get married and have lots of babies. Got it?"

Sam stared at her for a long moment, then leaned toward his brother and said in a loud whisper out of the corner of his mouth, "You married a crazy lady."

Sawyer's face split into a ridiculous grin that showed his latest bite of toast. "I know," he said. "But I look past it because she's so damn hot."

L.E. WAGENSVELD

# CHAPTER 5

"What about him?" Harper jerked her head in the direction of the table Charlotte had been serving. Setting down the tray of mugs, she stretched as if the weight had been unbearable. "He's cute."

Charlotte wrinkled her nose and studied the man at table ten. He came in once a month. Harper was right. He was cute, and she had noticed it before. Dark hair, kinked with a slight wave, fell above a pair of grey eyes. Charlotte sighed. "He's so... predictable. He always orders the same thing."

Harper raised her brows, confused. "So?"

"It's only that... when someone is so boring about their food choices, don't you think maybe they are the same way in other aspects of their life?"

"I've never thought that." Harper frowned. "Though now I might." She tapped one finger against her chin, her expression thoughtful. "Perhaps an experiment is in order."

Charlotte pretended she hadn't heard and went on. "Once table ten was occupied, so he left and came back when it was empty."

"That's a tad weird. But hey, we all are a tad weird." She elbowed Charlotte on the way to the coffeepot. "Some of us more than others. You'll get nowhere if you don't try."

"I try." She so did not try. With a sigh, Charlotte sucked at her bottom lip.

"How long has it been now since your 'wedding incident?'" Harper made air quotes around her words, penciled-on brows raised high.

"Three months."

"Geez, woman."

Three months since Sam had kissed her and splintered her entire view of their relationship. The man she had blithely considered a brother for over half her life had morphed into a sexual being Charlotte desperately wanted to kiss again. Then the next day, he was back, her old Sam, shy and awkward. He had never mentioned what had passed between them since, so she hadn't either.

Harper snapped her fingers in front of Charlotte's glazed eyes, and she jumped. "I'm beginning to worry about you. What if your vagina closes up from lack of use?"

"Oh, my God!" Charlotte hissed, glancing around to make sure no one had heard.

Harper crossed her arms and frowned. "Do you want me to tell Carmen what's going on?"

"Shit, no! Fine, I'll ask boring table ten out." Tossing a glare over her shoulder at Harper for good measure, Charlotte snatched the coffee pot and stalked across the café.

"Can I grab you anything else?" she asked when she reached the table. "More coffee?" She extended the pot and waggled her brows as the contents sloshed. "It's fresh."

"Well, in that case"—the patron, who may or may not be dull in bed, held his mug out to her with a lopsided grin—"but pour it slow so I can finally talk to you."

Charlotte faltered, losing a few drops of rich brown liquid over the rim of the cup.

"Finally? Have you tried it before?"

He nodded. "To no avail. You're always zipping around this place like Wonder Woman."

"I apologize. In the future, I'll attempt to be less

wonderful."

His laugh was sincere, and the timbre of it sent a pleasant sensation through her insides. She studied his face. His slate-grey eyes stood out against a rim of lashes so dark they were straight-up enviable. His jaw was square and clean-shaven. Charlotte couldn't help the niggling suspicion he spent more time in front of the mirror in the morning than she did.

"I wouldn't want to be responsible for the tragic decline of your wonderfulness." Fine lines fanned from the corners of his eyes when he smiled.

"My boss might ban you if he discovered you were behind it." Charlotte set his cup back down an inch from his hand and hugged the pot to her chest.

"Then I wouldn't be able to come in, sit in your section, and drink copious amounts of coffee, hoping to catch your attention.

"Hmmm, slightly creepy." Charlotte frowned. "Maybe a little stalkerish. Would this be a good time to tell you that you only get one free refill?"

"Then your friend over there must like me more than you do, and I owe this place a lot of money."

Charlotte sighed and shook her head. "She's too soft, that one. No stomach for rule enforcement."

"I'm glad the blame falls on her generosity and not my ability to be charming." His smile held just the right amount of self-deprecation for him to soften his words. "So, are you going to tell me your name, or should we just stick with Wonder Woman?"

"I believe someone claimed that moniker a long time ago."

"Hmmm, the real one, then? Or should we brainstorm another alias?"

"The real one, I suppose, though I see no reason I can't think of an alias if the fancy strikes."

He laughed, then raised a dark, expectant brow. "Well?"

"Well, what?" Charlotte asked.

31

"What is your name?"

"Charlotte. Charlotte Baker, though, speaking of alias, my friends have this lovely habit of calling me Chuck."

This time, both his brows shot up. "No way."

"I know, flattering, right?"

"My friends call *me* Chuck." He extended a hand to her, and Charlotte placed hers against his palm. It was smoother than she expected, but his grip was firm. "Charles Walston."

"So, the meeting of the Chucks." She couldn't help grinning at the absurdity, and she could admit Charles was pretty good at the playful banter for a boring guy. "I'm waiting for the lights to flicker mysteriously," she said.

They both glanced upward, and Charles laughed. "I'm sure the universe isn't overly concerned with us meeting. Somewhere the meeting of the two Sebastians, or Gabriels, is getting the monopoly on light flickering."

Charlotte let out a snort of laughter. "Why Sebastians or Gabriels?"

Charles shrugged. "One is a way cooler name than Chuck, and one is angelic. Plus, they were all I could think of on the spot. So, dinner tomorrow night?"

Charlotte twitched at the abruptness of the subject change. "I—" She glanced over to where Harper still hovered by the till, unabashedly staring at them before she nodded. "Yes. All right." Then, in her best shot at a game show host voice, "Let's make a date."

"You're totally weird, Charlotte Baker," Charles said. "I like it."

Leaving Charles laughing at the table, Charlotte scooped up the coffeepot and walked away.

\*\*\*

"Sam kissed me." Charlotte blurted, then squeezed her eyes shut while she waited for the resulting implosion. Harper could not blackmail her by telling Carmen if there was no secret to tell. The rationalization didn't quell the pounding of her heart.

Carmen had insisted on them both going for pre-honeymoon Mani-Pedis. Now, sitting in an overly white café off the spa, Charlotte had come to the uncomfortable realization she had to share the news with her friend.

Carmen spluttered on a swallow of latte and slammed her mug down, coughing until her face turned an alarming shade of crimson. "What?" she gasped. "When? How?"

Face hot, Charlotte lifted her drink, avoiding Carmen's wide eyes. "At your wedding. And the normal way, lips to lips. We were drinking. We danced. He was so nervous about his speech, I thought he'd implode. Then, afterward, we were at the bar, and he gave me this... this look." Goosebumps prickled along her arms.

Carmen leaned toward her. "What look?" she whispered.

"It was like he wasn't Sam anymore. At least not the Sam I've known for so long. He was a predator, and I was some little mouse."

Carmen snickered, then held up her hands. "I'm sorry! Just the analogy was fitting. You do squeak a lot."

"Do you want me to tell the story or not?" Charlotte glared at Carmen until she nodded, then leaned across the table. "It was electric. We were sitting there at the reception, and I didn't even care who was looking."

She took a deep breath. Flushed when the air stuttered and jerked over her lips. "He took my hand and kissed my wrist." She reached out and tapped the blue ribbon running beneath the surface of her friend's nearly translucent skin.

"Then he slid his hand over my knee, grabbed the back of my leg, and pulled me against him."

Carmen bobbed her head, never taking her rapt gaze from Charlotte's.

"Then he took my face in his hands—"

"Like, a chin cup? Or between the palms?" Carmen interrupted.

Charlotte reached up and cupped Carmen's smooth jaw in her palm. The warm press of Sam's fingertips against her pulse echoed in her memory. Somehow, knowing Sam as she did, she understood he had been monitoring her. He was reading and considering her reaction to him and his proximity. Both women ignored the slack-jawed stare of the man at the next table. "Like that, only all the way."

"Oh…" Carmen breathed. "That's sexy."

A high-pitched noise escaped Charlotte. A squeak of frustration or excitement, she wasn't sure. She clasped both hands over her mouth, realizing she had proved Carmen right. "I know," she whispered through her fingers. "Where the hell was I when Sam got sexy?"

Carmen gave her a pointed look but was kind enough not to voice the obvious.

"Did you notice? When you met him?" Charlotte asked, immediately regretting allowing the questions to slip out.

Carmen laughed. "I'm a terrible person to ask. I think all the Stevensons are sexy."

"Even Alice?"

"Especially Alice!"

Their laughter drew several looks, ranging from curious to annoyed. Both women sank lower into their chairs, ribs straining with contained mirth.

"What happened next?" Carmen skidded her chair around the table, so they sat side by side.

"We went to his room. I wanted… oh, man, I would have, but we didn't have protection."

Carmen's brow creased in puzzlement, "I thought guys always had one, like in their wallet in some secret condom pouch or something."

"So did I! But he didn't, and he went to look for one." Charlotte heaved a deep sigh. "Well, I was drunk and—"

Carmen gasped. "You threw up my wedding dinner?"

"No! You know me better than that!" Charlotte let out a deflating sigh. "I fell asleep."

"You fell asleep?" Carmen echoed in a perfect Rachel

Green impression before dissolving into another fit of laughter. "I'm sorry, I'm sorry." She waved a hand in Charlotte's face. "Go on."

"That's it. I woke up covered with a blanket. My shoes were off. Sam was on the other bed, sound asleep. I went to my room and got ready for breakfast. I was planning to talk to him, but he acted all weird and... and Sam-like."

"So, you guys haven't talked since?"

"No." Charlotte pulled her bottom lip between her teeth and gnawed. "I don't know what to think."

Carmen frowned. "You need to think about the fact you're dealing with Sam Stevenson. That man is capable of going full hermit if we don't keep an eye on him."

"This is true. I'm just... I don't know!"

"You're attracted to him. I can see it in your face; you're all puffy and pink."

"Holy crap on a cracker." Charlotte's cheeks flamed further, and she tried to hide behind a napkin. Carmen continued in gregarious ignorance of her friend's discomfort.

"Sam is good. Not to mention he's been in lo—" Carmen clamped her teeth on her lip, grinding the sentence to a halt.

Charlotte jerked her head around. "Excuse me? He's been what?"

Carmen grimaced and shook her head, her lips going white around the edges from the pressure she exerted in keeping them sealed.

"Carmen! What were you about to say?"

She clasped both of her hands across her mouth and stared at Charlotte, her eyes huge. Charlotte reached out and peeled Carmen's hands away. As if her fingers were the only force holding back the words, Carmen said, "He's been in love with you since you were teenagers."

"What!" Charlotte yelled, oblivious to the startled looks from around her. "What the hell are you talking about?"

Carmen glanced around, possibly searching for a hole to

crawl in and hide. "He's been crushing hard... for like ever." With sudden ferociousness, she brandished a finger at Charlotte. "Do not tell anyone that I told you! I'll get in so much trouble."

"Wait, how many people know?" Charlotte said, then tried to lower her voice. It was reaching unnecessary decibels. "How did you find out?"

"I noticed it the first time I saw you two together. Then last year, when we went camping, I may have overindulged and teased Sam about it... relentlessly until Sawyer made me go to bed. He said it has been a thing his family has known for years, but nobody talks about it, and I shouldn't either, least of all to you."

"You guys invited me on that trip, and I had to work."

Carmen nodded. "When Sawyer told him you weren't coming, Sam got all mopey. Like more than normal. He was quiet the entire weekend."

"And he... he admitted it was true? When you harassed him?" Charlotte's heart felt as if it was ready to climb out of her chest. It was a disturbing sensation, hanging on every one of Carmen's words as if they were about to change her life.

"Eventually, I think he only copped up because I already knew and admitting it was the only way he could get me to shut the hell up."

Charlotte frowned. "Why didn't he ever say anything to me?"

"Again, Chuck, let me reiterate. Because he is Sam."

"Still, it's been such a long time."

"He said when you guys were younger, he worried it would weird you out. Then stuff kept happening, and he knew how you felt about—" Carmen shrugged, her lily-white skin turning a dusty red that camouflaged her freckles. She didn't need to say her husband's name for Charlotte to understand all too well who she meant.

"Shit," Charlotte muttered.

"He figured it was better if he forgot about it." Carmen

held both her palms up, nose wrinkling. "Only he never did. Not really."

Charlotte blinked against the sudden burn of tears. In her mind, that night at the wedding had been fun and sexy, and it kindled a curiosity inside her. To know it meant so much more to Sam pained her. All this time, she'd been hurting him without knowing it.

"What do I do?" she whispered.

"Oh, honey." Carmen reached over and scooped up her hand. "First, you need to decide how you feel about all this. Then you need to talk to Sam. But above all else, don't start anything unless you are completely sure it's what you want."

"I hate that I hurt him and even didn't know." Charlotte's voice broke. She picked at the lace flowers of the tablecloth and waited for her vision to clear. Carmen made a tutting sound and pulled her into a one-armed hug.

"Sam is a big boy; he is as accountable for his actions as you. Don't worry about that. Decide what you need now before you do anything about Sam. I'm here to talk whenever you know that."

Charlotte sniffed and forced a smile on her face. "Once you get back from sexing it up all over the Bahamas, that is?"

Carmen nodded, a grin inching across her face. "Yes, after that."

Charlotte feigned a dark scowl. "You'll probably get knocked up and forget all about the rest of us."

Carmen reached out and patted her on the top of her head. "Probably."

L.E. WAGENSVELD

# CHAPTER 6

"What are you three cackling about?" Sam set his lunch on the table and slid onto the bench seat, bumping his shoulder against Deena's in greeting.

"Well, speak of the sweet-natured devil." Deena grinned and turned to Sam. "The girls and I were just saying we think you should set up an online dating profile."

Sam frowned. "Oh, God, like one of those *instant judgments, let's get laid* deals?"

"Doesn't have to be, though I'm sure you'd fare just fine on those as well." She patted his cheek with a calloused hand, "But there are more wholesome ones out there."

"Like what?" Sam frowned, "Christian Mingle? I literally just took the Lord's name in vain."

"You're swinging from one end of the spectrum to the other here, Sammy. There are lots of different options."

"Come on," Tasha piped up from the other side of the table. "Give it a go. What are you going to lose?"

"My dignity," Sam muttered. "Possibly my life. I'm an innocent, totally naïve; I could get cat-fished. I'm not entirely sure what that means, but I hear it's bad."

Tasha's eyes threatened to roll to the back of her skull. "We want to see you happy. And since you steadfastly refuse to date any of us… Well"—she held her palms up, dimples popping in her round cheeks—"here we are."

"You ladies have it all wrong. The only reason I refuse is I could never pick just one."

"Who says you have to?" Deena nudged him in the ribs as laughter erupted around the table.

Red-faced, Sam waited until his coworkers quieted. "Seriously, I'm happy. I don't know what makes you think otherwise."

"A man your age shouldn't be going from twelve-hour shifts, home to an empty apartment, back for another twelve, then back to an empty apartment… I'm sure you can see the pattern here, and let me tell you, it isn't healthy."

Sam scowled. "My life is fulfilling."

Deena's lips pursed, and she cocked her head at him. "Fulfilling, hey? What do you do for fun, Sam?"

Sam blinked at her. "What is this fun you speak of?" The sarcasm earned him a punch in the arm. "Lots of stuff!" He waved a hand in the air. "I walk dogs for the SPCA."

"And before bed every night, he polishes his halo," Tasha mumbled.

"How about sex? Hmm? Are you fulfilled in that department too?"

Sam closed his eyes against the urge to bury his face in his hands. The last thing they needed was more fodder to use against him. "You guys don't know everything about me." The argument sounded feeble even to his ears. "This is our workplace. I leave my personal life at home."

The three women raised their brows in synchronized doubt. Sam threw his hands toward the ceiling. "Fine. Sign me up." With a long-suffering sigh, he propped his chin in his hands. "At least find a decent site that doesn't cause all my morals to go up in smoke."

As one, the three women dove for their phones. Sara was the fastest draw. "Plenty of Fish? I hear good things about that one," she said. The other two women nodded in agreement, shifting in their seats so they could get a view of the minuscule screen.

"What's your full name?" Sara asked, her fingers flying.

"Why do they need that?"

Triple glares swiveled his way.

Sam held his hands up in surrender. "Samuel Sterling Stevenson."

"Of course, it is," Tasha muttered.

"Age? Thirty-four?"

Sam nodded.

"Height?"

"Six foot, four inches."

Sara typed, then paused. She glanced at the other women.

"What?" Sam growled, suspicion prickling at him.

"Are you interested in meeting women... or men?"

It took Sam a second or two to comprehend the question. "Are you asking if I'm gay?"

"Umm...Yes. Yes, I am."

"Well, well, well." Sam smirked. Crossing his arms, he leaned back in his chair. "Thought you guys knew everything about me?"

"Eight years, and it has only now occurred to me I've never actually heard you talk about a woman."

"Have you heard me talk about a man?" Sam laughed.

"Well, you mention your friend, Chuck, from high school once in a while."

Sam jerked upright in his chair. "Chuck is a girl! A woman. Her name is Charlotte. It's a joke."

Deena snorted. "I'm sure she thinks it's hilarious."

"People, people," Sara interjected. "We're burning through break time here. Am I checking female or male?"

"Female, if you please," Sam said.

They had nearly finished the profile when a thought occurred to Sam, "Wait, do you think that is why my mom pulled me aside last year and told me she'd love me no matter what?"

The others erupted into laughter. "Oh, Sammy boy."

Deena put an arm around his shoulder, squeezing him in a sideways hug. "I think so. That's lovely. I wish my mother had been that supportive of me when I came out. What did you say?"

Sam shoved down the pang of sadness at her words and shrugged. "I said, thanks, I love you too. I couldn't figure out why she was acting so weird. She said the only thing that mattered to her and my dad was that I found happiness."

Tasha shook her head, still shaking with barely restrained laughter. "Oh, you sweet, simple boy."

"My brother had just gotten engaged; I thought she was feeling sentimental." Sam snorted, then started to laugh as well, caught up in their amusement. Maybe they were right, and he was genuinely clueless.

"I don't understand how no one, man or woman—"

"Woman," Sam choked out, wiping his eyes with the back of his hand.

"—hasn't snatched you up yet."

Sam quieted and smiled at his friend. He couldn't help being touched by Tasha's seemingly genuine perplexity. "Despite your stubborn and, might I say, enduring affection for me, ladies, no lineups of any gender are waiting to knock down my door in their haste to date me."

"I think the problem lies in how you perceive the actions of the people you meet." Sara waved an encompassing arm at the busy cafeteria. "I could name at least three people in this room alone who've had or have the hots for you."

"Nonsense."

Sara held up a finger and began ticking off names. "Mary in X-ray, the PT… what's her name?"

"Trixie," Tasha supplied, her blue gaze travelling around the room.

"Oh, yeah." Sara grinned. "And Graydon, you worked nights with him a few times. He always asks about you."

"Sexy name. Still not interested in men."

"Oh!" Sara brandished her pointer finger at his face.

"Dr. Burke."

"Who?" Sam asked, blinking at her in surprise.

"The new doctor. Jane Burke."

"Yes?"

Sara froze, her eyes meeting Sam's and going wide. The four of them slowly turned around in their chairs.

"Hello, Dr. Burke." Tasha flashed her dimples, less pronounced now that her face resembled a tomato.

Dr. Burke tipped her head, a slight frown creasing the smooth skin between her fair brows. Blood crept up Sam's neck and flooded his face. He'd been giving Sara a hard time and knew who Dr. Burke was. Every red-blooded male in the hospital knew who Dr. Jane Burke was.

Tall and athletic, with brown eyes so sharp they seemed to see right into the root of a person when she spoke to them, she made Sam nervous. Uneasy in a way that wasn't entirely unpleasant.

"I couldn't help but overhear my name just now." She watched Sam as she spoke, one corner of her generous mouth curving the barest hint upward. Sam swallowed.

"Sara was telling Sam here he should ask you out for coffee." The point of Deena's elbow found Sam's ribs, and he flinched.

"Well, I don't drink coffee," Dr. Burke said, her gaze never leaving Sam's. Heat suffused his face, and he wondered if growing a beard would help hide the fact he was prone to blushing. Realizing they expected him to respond, Sam opened his mouth, but Dr. Burke interrupted him, a smile spreading across her lips. "I would, however, love to have dinner with you."

Ignoring the other women, Sam pulled himself together and stood. "I'm sorry. They took me a bit by surprise." He smiled, moving so he was standing in front of the doctor and blocking his coworkers' view from the table. "Dinner sounds great. I'm off Saturday?"

"I can make Saturday work."

"All right, well… great. That's great."

43

"I'll see you then."

She gave him another smile before turning, her head dipping back to the paperwork in her hand. Behind Sam, someone hissed, "Number!"

"Oh! Dr. Burke?"

She turned, chin tipped in question.

"Can I… I mean, I should grab your number, I guess?"

"Yes, you should." She unclipped the pen from her lanyard. "May I?"

Sam patted his scrub pocket, wincing. He had no paper, and his phone was sitting on the shelf in his locker. "Um."

Eyes twinkling, Dr. Burke took his hand in hers and flipped it over. The ball of the pen tickled the skin on the inside of his wrist as she scribbled the number.

"I think," she said, keeping hold of his hand a moment, "given the circumstances, outside of work, you could call me Jane." She squeezed his hand before releasing it. "Don't forget to write that down before you get back to work." Then she walked away, her long blonde braid dancing against the small of her back.

"Her posture is perfect," Tasha said in a reverent tone as the doctor left the room.

"Yeah, so is her posterior," Deena mumbled.

Shaking his head, Sam left the cafeteria without a backward glance.

\*\*\*

"Welcome home," Sam said after his brother released him from an unnecessarily long hug. Sawyer looked infuriatingly well. His skin was tanned dark gold, and the long strands of his blond hair had gone white under the tropical sun. Sam hated him, just a tiny bit. "You look… all right. The honeymoon was good?"

Sawyer flashed him a lecherous grin and jerked his head toward the bar. "Let's grab a beer, and then I'll tell you all about it."

"I'd rather you didn't," Sam muttered, following Sawyer. His bulk quickly parted the crowd that milled around the bartender. The bar had been Sawyer's idea. Sam invited his brother over for a beer at his apartment, but Sawyer had insisted they go out. It was Friday, and Sam had a rare Saturday off. The last thing he wanted, though, was to be hungover for his date with Jane.

"Okay, fine, only some details." Sawyer ordered for them, and Sam, without waiting for Sawyer, turned, and headed for a table in the far corner. Sawyer may have successfully gotten the introvert out of his cave, but Sam sure as shit would not sit right in the middle of all the bar's chaos.

They finished a round, chatting about the trip and the sights Sawyer and Carmen had seen. Sam talked little, but he was okay with listening to his brother tell his stories. Sawyer was so much like their mother, animated, gregarious, always ready to enthral listeners with a tale either true or made up if there was nothing to tell. He laughed more than he was used to. His cheeks actually hurt with it.

While he listened to Sawyer, Sam peeled the label off his beer bottle and created a tiny, neat pile on the table. He barely noticed he was doing it until Sawyer stopped talking and pointed at the debris. "What the fuck are you doing?"

"Uh." Sam looked at his bottle, then across at his brother. "I don't know. I have restless hands?"

Sawyer's brows rose, and his gaze flicked to Sam's face. "You know what they say about people who peel labels and shit like that, don't you?"

"No...but I have a strong feeling you are about to tell me."

Sawyer sat back and crossed his arms over his chest. "Apparently, it means you're sexually frustrated," he said smugly.

Sam snorted and lifted the bottle to his mouth, drinking deeply before setting it back on the table. A little harder than was strictly necessary. "Of course, I'm sexually frustrated!

45

I'm a socially awkward introvert who works eighty hours a week."

Sawyer rolled his eyes. "Get over yourself and go get laid."

Sam swallowed a rush of anger. Leaning his forearms on the table, he glared at his brother. "You know it isn't that easy for me."

"Why not!" Sawyer flung his hands up, then leaned forward, mimicking Sam's posture. "Surely you can figure out how to get a date."

Sam sighed. "Actually, for your information, I already have one. Tomorrow."

Sawyer slammed a palm down on the table. "Well, then what are you bellyaching about?"

"You realize, don't you?" Sam said, swinging a finger back and forth between them. "That you and I are as different as they come. I fell into this date by accident, and I'm nervous, all right? Casually dating beautiful women? This is your type of thing, not mine."

For a second, Sam thought he had stepped over a line. Sawyer's face darkened. He studied Sam for a long moment, then took a pull of his beer, setting it down slowly on the table before he said, "So, what's your thing then? Pining away for our childhood friend you're too chicken shit to talk to until you die?" He leaned forward, putting his finger so close to Sam's face, he was tempted to grab it and bend it back like they'd done as kids.

"Stop being so intense," Sawyer said. "Get out of your head. It's one date. Get laid for fuck's sake before your head... or your balls explode." With a look of pure exasperation aimed at Sam, he stood up from the table. "I'm going to grab us more beer."

Sam wanted to be pissed at Sawyer for what he'd said, but it wasn't as if his brother was wrong. He really needed to lighten up. He was going on a date with Jane, not marrying her. Sighing, he rubbed a hand over the back of his neck. "Okay, thanks... for the beer and the pep talk."

Sawyer smacked Sam's shoulder, then walked away. As he crossed the bar, half the women in the room swiveled their heads to follow his path. Still, Sawyer seemed utterly oblivious to the attention. Sam shook his head, chuckling softly to himself. His brother was really, truly blindly in love.

No sooner had the thought passed through his mind when Sam saw a familiar face that made the beer turn sour in his gut. *Celine.* Sawyer's ex-wife. Sam shot to his feet, some part of his brain telling him to run interference, but it was too late. Sam saw Celine's eyes narrow in Sawyer's direction. She turned and whispered in the ear of the woman she was with. Sam couldn't tell if it was the same one Celine had been cheating on Sawyer with, but at the moment, that seemed the least of their worries.

Celine and Sawyer had not had a clean break. After a late-term miscarriage, their marriage had eroded like a riverbank, chunks falling away in various torrents. The final straw had been when Sawyer learned Celine had been sleeping with a woman she worked with for nearly a year. The divorce had left a scar on his carefree, lighthearted brother. He was heavier after that, weighted down by the grief and guilt of it all. Sawyer had blamed himself for Celine cheating. He thought he had gone too far inside himself after the death of their child and hadn't given Celine the support she needed. They'd all tried to convince Sawyer none of it had been his fault, but Sam wasn't sure Sawyer had ever really believed them. It was a long time before he saw a hint of the old Sawyer. It wasn't until Sawyer had first told Sam about a woman he'd met. A woman named Carmen.

Sam still made a beeline across the bar, striving to cut Celine off, but she was tugging the other woman in Sawyer's direction. Sam saw the moment Sawyer's gaze landed on Celine. His features went blank and cold, a stillness that Sam had never seen before.

Sam reached Sawyer's side almost at the same time as Celine and her partner. Sawyer's only acknowledgment of

Sam's presence was to pass him the second beer he held. Sawyer raised the other one to his lips, took a long pull, then lowered it. "Celine," he said with a tip of his head. "Margot."

"Hey." Celine ran her gaze up and down the length of Sawyer, then cocked her head. "You look well." She gave Sam a cursory glance and a slight nod. The other woman, Margot, looked about as comfortable with the moment as Sam felt.

"Just got back from the Bahamas," Sawyer said.

"How nice. Old Dan actually let you take a vacation? You never got those when we were together."

"That's not true. He allowed it. When we went on our honeymoon," Sawyer said. It took a moment for the words to sink in, then Celine's gaze flicked down to Sawyer's ring finger.

"You got married." It wasn't a question. Sam noticed Celine's hand go to Margot's. "We are engaged too," she said in a rushed, too-high voice.

Margot's eyes snapped to Celine's face. "Wh——" she started, but Celine planted a firm kiss on her mouth, shutting her up.

"Congrats," Sawyer said, tipping his beer to them in a semblance of a toast. "When's the big day?"

Celine shrugged, still ignoring Margot's flabbergasted expression. "We haven't picked yet. We are just enjoying the glow of being engaged, you know?"

"Sure," Sawyer said. "And I'm enjoying the glow of a fucking great honeymoon with my beautiful wife. Cheers." He smashed the neck of his bottle, a little too hard, against the tumbler Celine held, then turned and walked away. Sam stood still for a second, looking between the two women's shocked expressions and Sawyer's retreating back. "Uh, well. Nice to see you, I guess," he said. Celine scowled, and Sam turned and followed his brother.

# CHAPTER 7

"Do you want to come up and have a drink?" Jane slid a hand over Sam's arm. Sam had enjoyed himself at dinner despite the thoughts of Charlotte winking at the edges of his consciousness. Jane was beautiful. With waves of glossy blonde hair falling down her back and her cheeks flushed pink from wine, she seemed younger, more carefree than she did when she was at work. Swallowing, he pushed away all thoughts of unruly dark curls and nodded.

"I'd like that." He turned his hand over and caught her fingers. She was tall. She only had to stretch an inch or so to press her lips against his. Sam had been bent slightly at the waist when he'd kissed Charlotte, even though she'd been on tiptoe. Sam growled at the memory and pulled Jane's lithe form against him, deepening the kiss, forcing thoughts of Charlotte from his mind. Charlotte didn't want him, and damn, he was sick of being lonely. He forced himself to remember Sawyer's words. This didn't have to be a big deal. It was a date. It was sex with another consenting adult.

Beneath his hands, Jane's body was foreign, long, slender, and firm. Sam skimmed his palms over her shoulders, down the length of her back, and gripped her ass cheeks. She let out a little whimper against his mouth, and he caught the sound, savoring it.

Plunging his tongue between her lips, Sam pressed harder, backing her toward the door of her apartment building. He was rough, but before he could slow down, Jane responded by twisting her fingers into the back of his hair until he hissed in pain. Heat unfurled down through Sam's limbs and straight to his groin in a painful stab.

When they broke apart, Jane pulled him through the door by the hand. Kicking off her shoes, she shoved the door shut with her foot without taking her eyes from his. "Make yourself at home. I'll pour us a glass of wine."

Sam stood in the entry, head tipped, observing the sway of her hips as she disappeared into the kitchen. Then he glanced around. The first word that came to mind was *sterile*. It was white. White walls with intermittent splashes of colour, primarily red. It reminded him of a scene from *Dexter*. Two white leather chairs sat a perfectly measured length from each other, and the pale wood floors reflected the light from the stainless-steel ceiling fixtures. The scene was like a wave of cold water on his neglected libido. He hoped she would bring white wine. Sam was not about to sit on anything in this room with a glass of red in his hand. It would terrify him.

An explosive sneeze echoed through the kitchen, followed by two more in rapid succession. "Sam?" Jane appeared, her brows inching up when she saw he was still hovering near the door. "Do you have a dog at home?"

"No." He stepped forward and tentatively accepted the glass of red wine she held toward him. As he brought it to his body, he kept a close eye on the liquid's proximity to the rim. "Do you?"

"No." Jane sniffed. "I'm extremely allergic. That's why I asked. My sinuses are staging a full rebellion."

"Oh." *Shit.*

"Oh?"

"Shit."

"Shit?"

"I volunteer at the SPCA on my days off. There must be hair on my jacket."

Jane stepped back so fast he may as well have announced he had Spanish influenza.

"I'm sorry." Sam held up his hands. "Can you take something?" It seemed wrong to ask, but hormones rushed through his body, insisting he attempt to salvage the evening.

Jane shook her head. "I have nothing for them. I ran out and don't have more."

"And presumably a person is safe in their own home from hostile dander intrusion." He groaned and smacked the heel of his hand gently against his forehead.

They stood in silence for a moment—well, Sam was silent. Jane sniffed and sipped her wine. Then she turned to him, her eyes taking on a twinkle. "Well, there's one thing that may help?" Her smile had a way of lighting her features. The often severe façade stretched and shifted to reveal a glimpse of the soul behind. There was a mischievous glint in her eyes. A shift in her posture told him it was an idea he would be on board with.

"What's that?"

"We could get you out of those clothes and into the shower."

L.E. WAGENSVELD

L.E. WAGENSVELD

# CHAPTER 8

"So, Chuck, tell me more about yourself. What do you do when you're not slinging breakfast at the yummiest place in town?" Charles leaned his forearms on the table, studying her. Charlotte picked at the warm circles of bread in the basket the server had set between them, trying to ignore his casual use of her nickname. She couldn't explain why it bothered her. She'd been the one to tell him about it.

"Nothing makes me go blank faster than a question like that," she admitted with a forced laugh. She pulled a deep breath and rolled her shoulders. "It's like that question is one of those old felt erasers and just wipes the chalkboard clean when someone speaks it." She mimed a wiping motion in front of her forehead.

Charles grinned. "At least I know you aren't too young for me since you remember chalkboard erasers." He settled back in the chair and gave her a gentle smile, seeming to pick up on her unease. "Let's start with the small stuff. I'll match you. Answer for an answer."

Charlotte jerked her head in a nod. "All right, shoot."

"What's your full name?"

"Charlotte Marie Baker. You?"

"Charles Thomas Walston."

Charlotte snorted. "How extremely English."

"Isn't it just? Parents were both from London. We came over when I was five. Your turn."

"My dad's side has been in Canada for decades, I suppose with a name like Baker. If we go back far enough, I've some English as well. My Mother was Cuban. She moved here and married my father when she was twenty-five."

Charles's smooth brow creased. "Was?"

"She... she passed when I was a couple months old."

"I'm sorry, Charlotte. Can I ask what happened?"

Charlotte closed her eyes. It wasn't until her twentieth birthday she learned the truth about her mother's death. The knowledge had done little besides unsettle her. She questioned things she'd never had cause to doubt before. "I'd rather not talk about that right now." She smiled to ease any rudeness in her words.

Charles nodded. "I understand."

The server returned to refill their waters and uncork the bottle of Malbec they'd ordered.

Charlotte took a hasty swallow as soon as the wine was in the glass in front of her. Then she resumed her assault on the bread, mind scrambling for small talk fodder.

Why was she so nervous? She wasn't a shy person by nature, but it had been eons since she'd been on a date. She took another drink, determined not to botch the evening.

"What do you do for a living?" She asked.

"I'm a lawyer."

That explained the smooth hands. "That must be exciting."

"I deal with a lot of parking ticket disputes, questioning people about their divorces, and listening to people arguing about minuscule amounts of money." He flourished his hand in the air in a motion like he was writing. "Sometimes people pay for my signature. It really gets the blood pumping."

"Well, it's always great to be passionate about what you

do."

Charles snorted, deftly turning the conversation back to Charlotte. "Tell me about your passions. Is serving food one of them?"

"In a way. Food is, definitely." Charlotte chewed at her bottom lip. "What I really want is to open my own bakery."

He nodded, indicating that she should keep talking.

"A small place. With daily specials that people line up for in the morning. And a kick-ass cup of coffee, of course."

"Amen to that."

"And when the shelves are empty, I'll plaster a sign on the door saying we're closed for the day. People will forgive my eccentric and quirky business habits because of how mind-blowing my products are."

"I think it's a great idea. There is no doubt in my mind you would pull it off."

"Thanks, I wish I could say the same."

"What are you scared of?"

Charlotte gave a wry laugh. "Gee, I don't know. Failure, humiliation, bankruptcy. To name a few."

"And if none of those worst-case scenarios came true?"

"Then I'd be living the dream, wouldn't I?" Charlotte said with a grim smile.

Charles raised one of his dark brows. The expression clearly expressed he thought her answer was right there in her question.

"I'll tell you what." He took a sip of wine, then smiled across the table. "You make gluten-free brownies, and you'll have at least one loyal customer for life."

"Gluten-free?" Charlotte gasped, clutching her hand to her chest.

Charles hung his head. "Alas, it is true. I'm one of 'them.' Is that a deal-breaker?"

"It could be." Charlotte spun the stem of her wineglass between her fingers. "I have to be honest; you've moved down the list a few notches."

"Hmm." Charles's face remained thoughtful, but there

was a playful twinkle in his eyes. "I better step up the old romance game to come back from this one."

"Wait, a damn minute." Charlotte glanced down at the empty breadbasket. "Does that mean I ate all the bread?"

\*\*\*

He kissed her goodnight. A pleasant enough kiss. Firm and expertly timed. Charlotte closed her eyes, waited for her toes to curl in her shoes and her heart to skip and bump against her ribs. A gentle furl of warmth uncurled in her belly, but that was the extent of it. No fireworks. No fading of the world around them. Charles paused, probably waiting for an invitation upstairs, but Charlotte only smiled and squeezed his arm.

"Thank you again. That was nice. I had a lot of fun."

A slight shadow of disappointment crossed Charles's grey eyes. "It was. Though I was going for more than nice." He smiled to show he was kidding, but it didn't reach his eyes. "Can I call you?"

"Yes, please do." Maybe next time, once they knew each other better, things would improve. Maybe she wouldn't be so awkward. A little nagging voice that sounded suspiciously like Carmen popped up in the back of her mind. Maybe Charles would turn into Sam, and then all would be well. Charlotte mentally told the voice to stuff it and smiled. "Well, good night."

"Goodnight, Chuck."

Again, the nickname rankled her. That name had people who were allowed to use it, the Stevensons, Carmen—not strangers. She shook her head as she walked up the stairs to her apartment. What was wrong with her?

When she got out of the shower, there was a text from Carmen waiting.

*Please report on the date.*

Shaking her head, Charlotte punched out a quick response.

*Pleasantly mediocre.*

She dreamed of Sam that night. His silky curls and the rasp of his five o'clock shadow as he ran his lips down her neck and chest. Around midnight, she came awake with a gasp, the images blazing behind her lids and her body trembling. "Son of a bitch," she muttered and stuffed her face into her pillow.

L.E. WAGENSVELD

# CHAPTER 9

"We are all doing Christmas at Dan and Alice's this year. Did they tell you?" Carmen inhaled the steam from her cup and sighed. "I love coffee," she murmured, more to the mug than to Charlotte.

Charlotte chuckled and propped a hip against the table where Carmen sat. "Heck ya, Sista."

Carmen cocked her head, tearing her eyes away from her cup long enough to glance at Charlotte. "To the question or the statement?"

"I concur with both. October is a tad early to be talking about Christmas, though, isn't it?"

"Christmas at the Stevensons' is the best time of the year. No reason we shouldn't be excited about it."

Charlotte nodded. "Alice is the queen of Christmas. She gave me the first Christmas present I remember getting. A stuffed Care Bear. I still have him on my bed. He's a little worse for wear, and he's seen things he shouldn't have been privy to, but old Tender Heart has been a constant companion these long years."

"Ah, Care a Lot. Those were simpler times." Carmen sat back in her chair. "You're mentally prepared to see Samuel, then?"

"As prepared as I ever will be. Not sure if I'll punch him in the face or jump his bones in front of everyone." She shrugged. "It's anyone's guess if you'd like to get ahead of the game and start a betting pool now."

"Please don't do either. Well, you can jump his bones but not in front of us. I, unlike Tender Heart, have a say in the matter, and I don't wish to be subjected to that."

"Time will tell, my friend." Charlotte stabbed a fork into Carmen's omelette, glanced around the café, then scooped a healthy bite into her mouth. "Why can't I get this figured out?" she mumbled.

Carmen gave her a look that clearly said, *because you're an idiot, that's why,* but out loud, she said, "Because you refuse to talk to the man like a normal adult."

Charlotte tapped a finger against her chin. "I don't see the issue."

Carmen released a long-suffering sigh. "I didn't think you would. That would just be asking, too. Oh——" She jerked her chin toward the other side of the restaurant. "That man is trying to get your attention."

Speed chewing another stolen bite of eggs, Charlotte turned to the man in the corner with his back to the wall. "What do you want?" she barked, then flashed the old-timer a grin.

"Hey, kid, you going to chat all day, or are you going to get back to work?"

"How many times do I have to tell you I'm not a kid?"

"Uh-huh, all I know is, I've got socks older than you."

"You should buy new socks," Charlotte countered, "and why do you even need the coffee? I've seen how much cream and sugar you pour in there. You may as well have a milkshake."

The man grinned, his eyes nearly lost in the wrinkles and mirth that changed his entire countenance. "Don't be mean to me. I'm old and feeble."

Charlotte rolled her eyes but couldn't keep the smile from inching across her face as she turned back to Carmen.

"So, are you going to see him again?" Carmen asked around a bite of toast.

"Who?" Charlotte grabbed for the straggling tendrils of her friend's train of thought. "Charles?"

"Yeah."

"I don't know, we've been out three times now, and it's not bad, it's just—" Charlotte shrugged, letting her words float away.

"It's not what it was with Sam?" Carmen supplied after a moment.

Charlotte sighed. "It's not what it was with Sam."

\*\*\*

Charlotte said goodbye to Carmen and cleaned up the aftermath of the breakfast rush. Her mind kept leaping between thoughts of Sam and Charles.

"Hey, Charlotte, the phone is for you." Harper waved her over, passing Charlotte the handset and taking the cloth from her hand to tend to the tables Charlotte had abandoned.

"Hello, this is Charlotte."

"Chuck? Honey, it's Alice."

A rock-hard ball of worry formed in Charlotte's stomach at the tension in Alice's voice.

"Alice, what's wrong?"

"It's your dad. He was here with Dan, and—" A shuddering breath sounded over the line. "He collapsed. We called the ambulance. The paramedics thought it was a stroke, but they couldn't tell us for sure."

Bright pinpoints of light darted across Charlotte's vision. Harper said something to her, alarmed, but the words and her concerned face faded in and out of focus.

"Is he... will he—" Charlotte choked out before her voice broke.

"We don't know, sweetie. I'm coming to get you now. I didn't want to tell you on the phone, but I thought you would need the time to speak to your boss."

With a promise to arrive in a few moments, Alice disconnected. Charlotte stared at the handset, the Stevensons' familiar number still blinking on the screen. Harper reached out and took it from her, settling it in the cradle.

"Go, sit down." With an arm around her waist, Harper guided Charlotte to a chair. "I'll talk to Gary and get you covered."

Tremors had started in her hands, and no amount of clenching would quell them. She stared at her pink-tipped nails, watching how they bit into her palms. She didn't hear Alice enter the café, but when the older woman's arms wrapped around her shoulders, she turned her face into the older woman's shoulder.

Alice held her for a moment, then tugged her to her feet. "Come on, honey." Alice led her to the car, emitting a running stream of dialogue the entire way. Anchoring herself to Alice's voice, Charlotte laid her head against the glass of the car window and closed her eyes, willing the drive to pass quickly.

# CHAPTER 10

"Well, hello there. If it isn't my second-favourite nurse."

"Hello, Mr. Edwards. How are you today?" Sam grinned at the older man as he pushed the med cart into the room.

"Sorry to deprive you of Deena's company, but you're stuck with me today. How are you feeling?"

"Ahh, well. You know. All right for a dying man." Mr. Edwards shifted on the bed. Every one of his movements had slowed in the last few weeks. The flesh was melting from his massive frame right before Sam's eyes. Deep purple bags pillowed his sparkling blue eyes, but Sam knew as long as mischief still existed in that gaze, it wasn't yet time to worry.

"Can I do anything for you?" he asked.

"As long as you keep bringing those drugs, lad, I'll be all right."

Sam forced another smile. When he passed over the cup of water, he used the motion as an excuse to draw the blankets up around Mr. Edwards's chest. "You can count on me for that. It's actually in my job description."

"Have I shown you the new batch of pictures yet, Sam?"

"No, I don't believe you have."

"Do you have a moment? I know you're a busy man."

"For new pictures? I've got all the time in the world," Sam said, and he meant every word. It was people like Mr. Edwards that made Sam feel it was all worth it. The long hours, and the lack of sleep or social life. Giving these people even a sliver of what they needed to be happy in their final days was worth every sacrifice Sam made.

Sam waited while the older man finished his cup of pills and then took his phone from under his pillow.

"Got them all here on the cell phone. Didn't want the thing when the kids gave it to me, had no clue at all what to do with the damn thing, but now I'm not sure what I'd do without it."

Sam chuckled. "I can relate."

"They all send me photos on it, every day. I've got three daughters and eight grandkids. They all live hours away, but they keep close tabs on me. When it gets to the end... they'll be here."

Sam leaned over, watching as one gnarled, snub-nailed finger swiped through the photos. Kids of varying ages scrolled past, their faces smiling. Then the big heart-melting eyes of a droopy-faced black dog. Mr. Edwards froze, his finger poised over the screen. Sam glanced at his face. The sadness in the man's eyes sent a spike right into Sam's heart.

"If there is one thing I regret," Mr. Edwards said, then cleared his throat, "one thing I regret is I won't get to say goodbye to this guy."

Sam swallowed, but any words he may have spoken remained stuck in his throat. He gave a jerky nod.

"Had him nine years this fall." Mr. Edwards gave a bitter bark of laughter. "Won't have too many left in him either, poor old boy."

"I'm sure he's had a wonderful life." Sam's voice was husky. He reached out to straighten the different objects on the nightstand.

"Oh, yeah, he's living the high life at my buddy's place, playing with all his grandchildren." Mr. Edwards grinned down at the photo. The tip of his finger rested on the dog's glossy head for a moment, and then he clicked off the screen.

"Thanks for taking the time to listen to an old man, Nurse Sam."

"Anytime." Sam held his hand out. Mr. Edwards's large grip engulfed it. Still strong, he squeezed Sam's between both of his. "You have a good day, Mr. Edwards," Sam said.

Sam gathered his things and started the cart toward the door. When he glanced back, Mr. Edwards's balding head was tucked against the pillow, his breathing gentle. Sam stepped back across the room, eased the phone between the slack fingers, and set it on the bedside table. When he was through the door, he stopped and rested his back against the doorjamb, letting his head drop. It took a few deep breaths before the band around his chest eased away.

"You all right, Stevenson?" One of the doctors stood down the hall, files in hand. He cocked his head, throwing Sam a suspicious look.

"Dr. Farley, good morning. Yes, I'm fine."

Dr. Farley's brown eyes went to the number on the door. Understanding dawned on his face. "Mr. Edwards." He gave Sam a half-smile. "He's a great guy. Did he show you photos of the dog?"

Sam shoved a hand through his hair. "Yes, just now."

Farley bobbed his head. "That explains the look." He clasped Sam on the shoulder as he passed. "You're doing a good job, Stevenson."

"Thank You, Doctor."

*** 

"Hey, Sam?"

Sam turned, holding his soap-coated hands out in front of him. "Yeah?"

"I've got a young lady asking if you're on shift. Came in

with her father. Stroke victim."

Sam frowned, anxiety fizzing in his chest and exhaustion weighing across his shoulders. His twelve-hour shift had ended an hour ago. "Did she give you a name?"

"Yeah." The nurse's lined brow wrinkled further, perplexed. "*She* said Chuck?"

Sam froze. His heart picked up speed with enough force that his head spun.

"Stevenson, you're dripping on the floor."

"Shit!" Sam plunged his hands back into the stream of water, hissing at the heat. "Is Ms. Baker all right?" he asked over his shoulder, but the nurse had already disappeared through the swinging doors of the scrub room.

Using his elbow to bang out a bundle of paper towels, Sam dried his hands. He wished there was a mirror, but he knew what he would see. Blue eyes accented by dark circles. Blond hair in disarray and long overdue for a trim. He rubbed his hand across his jaw. A trim and a shave. He'd never liked to wear a beard. It always came in two shades darker than his hair. As if the stubborn genes of his parents had done battle and then had come to a compromise.

Shaking his head, Sam turned and pushed through the door and into the bright hallway. What was he doing? Charlotte needed him, and he was standing here worried about how he looked.

"Mr. Baker is in room twenty-nine"—the receptionist's fingers flew over the keyboard in a symphony of taps and clicks— "admitted two hours ago."

Sam sucked a breath through his teeth. "Thanks, Mary." His heart was pounding. He broke into a jog, his runners squeaking as he rounded a corner. Room Twenty-Nine was on his left. In the hall between him and the room, Charlotte paced until she reached door thirty-four, turned, and started back. Her arms were wrapped around her middle, her body folded in on itself as if in physical pain, the glossy curtain of her curly dark hair hiding her face.

Sam pulled in a deep breath. It had been nearly three

months since he had laid eyes on her. Not even a glimpse since he had made an idiot of himself at the wedding.

She looked up then, sensing him, her face tear-streaked and blotchy. The sight of her broke Sam's heart. A hiccupping sob broke free when she met Sam's eyes. Without a word, she rushed straight to him. He caught her, crushing her against his chest.

"Oh, Sam." When he finally set her down, she stepped back and wiped her nose on the cuff of her hoodie. Hours of tears had left wandering paths over her cheeks.

"I'm so glad you're here. Everyone is asking questions, and I... I'm scared, Sam."

She seemed even smaller than usual, somehow, as if her fear had caved her in. Fear filled her eyes, and he couldn't help himself. He pulled her back against his chest, encircling her with his arms, wishing he could protect her.

"It'll be all right," Sam said against her hair. "Chuck, your dad is tough as nails, and they got him here quickly. Time means everything with a stroke."

Her arms rose and wrapped around his waist. She nodded against his chest. "You're right. You must be right, right?"

"Right." He gave her one more squeeze than set her back a step, keeping one hand on her arm, tipping his head so she was forced to meet his eyes. "What can I help with? Are you hungry?"

"I guess. I haven't eaten since this morning at work— Oh!" She clapped a hand against her brow. "Work. I have to call them. What time is it?"

"I think around midnight."

"Midnight?" Charlotte squeaked.

He glanced around. Most of the rooms had clocks, but in an age where everyone carried cell phones, fewer of them seemed to hold consistent time. "I'm pretty good at guessing after all these years."

Charlotte moaned and buried her face in both hands. "I can't believe it has only been a few hours. This is a nightmare."

"Hey, look at me." Sam seized her shoulders, holding her still. "Why don't I sit with him? You go leave a message for work. Wash your face and grab a hot tea and a snack. Do what you need to do to get yourself feeling a little more settled. All right?"

He could not keep himself from touching her. One hand rubbed her arm until she nodded. Worry over her well-being chased away any thought of his own exhaustion. "You can't take care of him if you don't take care of yourself first. It's going to be a long night, but I'm going to be here with you the whole time."

Charlotte sighed. "Yes, you're right, I guess. You'll call me, though, if anything changes?"

"The exact second it does. I won't take my eyes off him."

Tears filled her eyes once more when she met his gaze, but she blinked them away with a fierce scowl. "Thank you, Sam." Before she turned away, she clasped his hand in hers, squeezing it until his knuckles protested. Then, her spine straightening, she started down the brightly lit hallway.

# CHAPTER 11

Charlotte stood from the hard plastic chair and stretched. She needed to move. She needed to breathe before she went crazy in the stale, antiseptic air full of so many beeps and hums. Three days in the room, waiting in an endless limbo, were more than she could handle. A glance at the bed suffused her with guilt. Though he was still pale, her father looked peaceful. His chest rose and fell in a steady, comforting rhythm.

Charlotte bent and pressed a kiss to his wrinkled brow. "I'll be right back, Papa. Behave yourself, no flirting with the nurses."

She hurried out of the room before she could change her mind. As she walked down the white halls, she stretched her neck and rolled her shoulders in circles. Vertebrae cracked, and muscles sang out with the stiffness of misuse. The ropes of strain pulled all the way to the base of her skull. Sighing, she resigned herself to do more. Maybe she would see if Carmen was up for a yoga class tonight. She rejected the thought almost instantly.

She was about to step into the cafeteria when the rumble of a familiar laugh stopped her. Charlotte peeked around the corner. Sam stood across the room, one shoulder propped against the wall, a bottle of water dangling from his fingers. At the table in front of him were two nurses in scrubs and an older woman dressed in smart office attire.

"Eventful morning, Sammy?" One nurse, a brunette in her mid-fifties, grinned up at Sam as she sipped her coffee.

"I've got to admit," Sam said, wrinkling his nose. "I thought it was only when you ladies were on shift that Mr. Crawley forgot his gown, but he proved me wrong. It may be eight in the morning, but it was a full moon in that room."

"That's really the first time you've started your day with an eyeful of pancake butt?"

Sam took a long pull of water, then capped it, smirking. "Before today, only the one in the mirror."

The women all sniggered. "Darling, scrubs don't lie. That ain't no pancake butt."

Sam's cheeks went pink, but he laughed.

Charlotte's mouth went dry. It was like witnessing a Sam she had never met. A Sam in his element, his comfort zone. She realized she didn't know him as well as she'd thought. He always kept a level of his defensive wall up, even with her. The thought made her stomach ache.

"Maybe you should dress as Mr. Crawley for Halloween, Sam." The brunette gave him an exaggerated wink.

Sam threw back his head and laughed. "Do I need to go fill out a report with HR?" He had one dimple on his cheek that only showed when he smiled a certain way. It was a trait Sam shared with his brother. Charlotte had seen it on Sawyer many times, fewer on Sam. Once, she'd even witnessed the dimple on Dan, the ill-fated time he shaved his goatee. The mark of the Stevenson men.

Someone came around the corner, forcing Charlotte to step into view. One woman sitting by Sam caught her eye.

"Sammy, isn't that your friend?" The woman stood and beckoned for her to join them. Charlotte drew a deep breath, forcing a smile before walking toward the table.

At her sudden appearance, Sam straightened. He shoved

his free hand through his hair and flashed her a sweet smile. "Hey, Chuck. How are you?"

The head of every woman at the table swiveled in his direction. "Chuck?" They parroted.

Sam flapped a hand in at them. "It's a long story." Turning his back on them, he stepped closer to Charlotte, tipping his head to study her face. "Is your dad all right?" One hand rose and hovered at her elbow, almost touching her before it dropped back to his side. "Are you all right?"

"Dad is fine, given the circumstances. They say things are looking better, but they still can't really say for sure." She paused as the sudden urge to cry caught her by the throat and squeezed.

"And you?" Sam prodded.

"I…" Charlotte swallowed. "I'm just—" Her voice broke, and the breath she drew shook.

Sam's eyes creased in the corners. The hand rose again, and this time, it cupped her elbow. Heat seeped from his palm and through the material of her sweatshirt, soaking her skin. Sam squeezed gently, as if he could share his strength with her by pressing it through the layers.

"You're exhausted."

It seemed like a betrayal to her father to complain about over-tiredness. She settled for a nod.

"Are you driving back today?" Sam asked.

"Yes. I was going to leave in an hour or so. Go home for a bit and try to sleep."

Using the hand on her arm, Sam drew her away from curious ears. "I want you to go stay at my place."

"Oh, no, I can't ask—"

"You're not, I'm telling you." His gaze moved over her, assessing her. "I'm not comfortable with you driving alone, upset, and sleep deprived."

Charlotte blinked at him. She should say no, but he was right. Exhaustion weighed at her limbs, and the prospect of the drive home and the emptiness of her apartment upon arrival yawned before her like a crevasse Charlotte was not ready to face. She took a second to study Sam. His jaw had a stubborn set to it she had seen before, and worry darkened his eyes. There was no use arguing. "All right. Just for a day or so," she conceded. She didn't want to be an hour away, not while things were still uncertain about her dad, but she needed to shower and put on clean clothes before they kicked her out for stinking up the place.

Sam slipped an arm around her shoulder. "Come on. I've got a few minutes left on my break. Let's get my keys."

"All right," she repeated, following him out of the cafeteria and down a short hallway to a room lined with lockers. "So, is this your phone booth?" she asked, watching Sam's long fingers spin a combination on the lock in front of him.

"Hmmm?" He turned to her; one tawny brow raised in question.

"Your phone booth? Where you switch your identities?" When he stared at her blankly, Charlotte smacked the heel of her hand against her forehead. "Oh, Sam." For the first time in days, laughter bubbled up inside her. "Clark Kent, Superman? Changes in a phone booth…"

"Oh, yeah, I gotcha." He chuckled and turned back to the locker, swinging the door open with a creak.

"You know who Superman is, don't you?" She poked him in the ribs, and he flinched away with a sound that, to his shame, could only be called a squeal.

"Of course, I know who Superman is!"

"What's that?" Charlotte squeezed in beside him, squinting at the photo stuck to the inside of the metal door.

"Oh, ah…" Colour suffused his cheeks, and he snatched the keys off the shelf and tried to shut the locker before she could make it out.

"Let me see!" She caught the door and nudged him out of the way. "Oh, my God."

Sam scowled down at her. "It's an excellent picture. Mom gave it to me."

Stuck with a wad of blue sticky tack was a print of four

teenagers.

Sawyer and Charlotte, about fifteen, squatting beside a fluffy black dog. Petite Sasha, her pale features bright with laughter, stood behind her younger brother, one hand on his shoulder. And Sam, arms crossed, slightly apart from the group. The air of nineteen-year-old superiority he eluded was ruined by the turned-up corner of his mouth and the twinkle in his eyes. Eyes that weren't looking into the camera but down at the pair hugging the dog.

"Oh, it's BamBam!" Charlotte reached a finger to touch the dog's grinning face. "He was the best dog."

Sam smiled, putting his finger next to hers on the tip of the lolling pink tongue. "I still miss that mutt."

"You always loved dogs so much. Why don't you have one?"

Sam sighed. "It wouldn't be fair." With a sad shake of his head, he shut the locker door. "I'm never home. That's no life for a man's best friend."

"I guess." It struck Charlotte suddenly how lonely Sam must be.

"There's a man in hospice, and he has this dog—" He stopped talking, his eyes clouding, and his face scrunched at whatever he was remembering. "Never mind."

Charlotte cocked her head but didn't press him. Whatever he meant to say brought a flash of such sadness to his expressive eyes. Charlotte wasn't sure she could bear to hear it at the moment.

"Do you remember where my apartment is?" he asked, changing the subject.

She bobbed her head. "I think so."

He gave her the address anyway. Then he took her hand in his and placed the key on her palm, closing her fingers around it. His hands were warm, slightly rough as they grazed the skin on the back of her hand. The hair along her arms rose, and the memory of his lips on her wrist bubbled to the surface. Charlotte suppressed a shiver. When she glanced up, he was studying her face. Blue eyes darkened as his gaze slid from hers and down, slowly, until they reached her lips.

Heat rose off his lean body in waves. He smelled so distinctly Sam. Spicy deodorant and antiseptic soap with a hint of something more. Something visceral and male. Charlotte's heart pounded in response.

The column of Sam's throat worked. The tip of his tongue flicked across his lips, and unconsciously, Charlotte mirrored the action. She moved closer to him as if her body closed the gap without her brain's permission.

"Code White! ER, available staff, please respond."

Sam's entire body flinched. "Shit!" He grabbed the lanyard at his neck and spoke into it rapidly.

"I have to go." Squeezing her upper arm, he frowned at her, brows drawn in with concern. "Will you be all right?"

"Of course." Charlotte's voice emerged as little more than a doubtful whisper.

Sam spun away. "Make yourself at home and get some rest!" he called as he jogged out of the room.

\*\*\*

"What the—?" Sam eased the door to his apartment open and slipped inside. Every light in the place was on, and the scent of fresh baking emanated from the kitchen to torment him.

"Chuck?" he whispered, kicking off his shoes. "Are you up?"

No reply came from the living room. Sam's socked feet whispered across the wood flooring as he crept down the hall. Charlotte was curled up on the couch, sound asleep, wrapped in the blanket from the back of the chair. With a pang, Sam realized he never told her where to find the extra bedding. Shaking his head at his oversight, Sam went up to his room. Visitors were a rarity in his home. Hell, he was barely here.

Taking the second pillow off his bed, he reached into the

closet and felt around on the shelf. There had to be something. His fingers came across soft cotton, and he pulled the fabric free. It was the quilt his mother made him when he was a baby. All of Alice's children had one. Bright squares of cloth, with names and dates embroidered across the centre. She had learned to quilt when she was pregnant with Sam. On his blanket, the words were blocky and sprawling. Sasha's had been an improvement, and Sawyer's near perfection. Smiling, Sam brought the blanket to his nose. It held the faint scent of dust, but nothing serious. A few shakes to free the motes, and he carried it to the living room, spreading it as best he could over Charlotte without jostling her.

On the kitchen counter, he discovered the source of the delicious aroma. A plate stacked high with round, fat muffins sat on the table. Beside the pile was a folded square of paper. He opened it.

*You're too skinny. Eat some muffins and get some sleep.*
*P.S. Thank you*
*Xoxo*

"Bossy." Sam grinned and snagged two from the pile, glancing over his shoulder in the couch's direction. More than anything, Sam wished he could wake her up. He wanted to share the details of the evening and to hear her laugh. Halfway through the first muffin, Sam realized he'd wandered back into the living room. One hand moved toward her shoulder before he stopped himself. Charlotte mumbled in her sleep and cuddled her face into the satin trim of the quilt. Blue rings of exhaustion extended past the black crescents of her lashes. Silken curls clung to her lips. Sam reached a finger out and slid the hairs back, tucking them behind the curve of her ear. Sucking a deep breath, he backed away from the couch. Watery, dull light from the window danced on the planes of her cheek, emitted by the open curtains. Sam crossed the room and pulled the blinds closed, blanketing the place in the inky darkness.

# CHAPTER 12

"Sam, if I'm going to blow your mind with these ribs, I need that slow cooker. You assured me you had one, and I, in all my naivety, trusted you."

Charlotte stood in Sam's kitchen, launching into the rant as soon as he stepped through the door, yawning.

"Good morning to you too." Pausing, he studied her for a moment, attempting to ignore the little thrill of happiness her presence caused. She'd been there for three days, and already it felt natural to come downstairs and find her. Sam stretched his arms over his head, yawning again, so hard his jaw cracked. Then he crossed the room to peek over Charlotte's shoulder. "You really should wave a wooden spoon at me during this tirade. It would complete the scene."

She turned to scowl at him. "If I had a wooden spoon in my hand, I'd be beating you over the head with it until I got the slow cooker I was promised." She took a menacing step toward the utensil jar on the counter.

Sam laughed and held up his hands. "All right, all right. I think it's in the hall closet, in a box still. I got it as a Christmas gift a few years ago."

Charlotte stared at him wordlessly until he shifted from

foot to foot. Then she turned and left the kitchen, muttering under her breath. Sam went to the counter where Charlotte had been working and picked up the knife, beginning to dice the tomatoes she'd abandoned.

"What the hell is this?" Charlotte's voice floated down the hall a few moments later.

"What's what?" Sam set the knife down and wiped tomato juice on a towel. Charlotte's head popped around the corner.

Smirking, she held up a green leather tunic. "What's this?"

"Shit!" Sam snatched for it, but Charlotte jumped back.

Sam made another grab for the tunic, but Charlotte dashed away, her grin reflecting in her eyes. "Tell me! Tell me!" she sang, scooting around in circles, keeping the island between them. Sam attempted to dive across, using his height to grab her.

A thoughtful look crossed her face. "Oh, my God. Is there more?" When Sam shook his head hard, she let out a wicked laugh and tossed the garment square into his face before making a break for the hall. Blinded, Sam snaked out an arm in one last attempt, snagging her around the waist. She slithered out of his grip and raced away. Sam heard her rifling around as he untangled himself.

"Hey!" Using the door frame as leverage, he darted after her, slipping across the wood floors. "You brat! You are just as big a brat now as you always were," he yelled. "Have you never heard of privacy!"

She answered by yanking the rest of his costume, a hooded cloak and rough-spun trousers with a wide belt, complete with sword and sheath, out of the closet.

"This is the best day ever!" She cackled, turning the garments over, running them through her fingers before directing the full power of her smile at him. Sam nearly forgot the crippling force of his embarrassment under its radiance.

"Tell me what you do with these." She put her hands

together beseechingly. "Please, Sam. I'll never ask anything of you again."

He considered denying everything. Saying they were an old Halloween costume, or they weren't his at all. He didn't.

"I have been known… on the rare occasion that I have the time… to LARP," he whispered, forcing the words past the nearly overpowering urge to go hide in a hole.

Charlotte blinked at him. "What in the actual hell is LARPing?"

Sam studied the patterns and whorls in the wood flooring. "Live. Action. Role. Play," he mumbled.

"Is that like… a sexual thing?" Charlotte asked, staring at the clothing in her hands as if considering tossing it to the floor. "Like… furries?"

Sam squeezed his eyes shut. "What the hell are furries?" he groaned.

"You know, people who dress up in costumes like stuffed animals and… do stuff." Turning back to the closet, she laid the costume across a basket and wiped her hands on her jeans. "I mean, each to their own. I don't judge."

Sam pressed the bridge of his nose between his thumb and pointer finger until stars danced across his vision. "My God, Chuck, do you really think—"

Charlotte held her palms up. "Hey man, it's always the quiet ones."

Sam groaned and slid his back down the wall until he sat on the floor. "It's just for fun. You remember how much I love fantasy novels and history, well—" He gestured toward the costume. "A friend introduced me to it a few years ago. It's freeing. Allows you to forget who you are and get lost in a fantasy for a bit."

Chuck stared at him as if he'd sprouted an extra head, but finally, she nodded slowly. "I can see that, I suppose."

Sam narrowed his eyes. Raising a finger, he brandished it at her. "If you ever tell anyone, especially my brother, Charlotte Baker, I'll—"

She crossed her arms and scowled, daring him to

continue. "You'll do what, Stevenson?"

One corner of Sam's lips hitched upward. Slowly, he allowed the grin to spread across his face. "I'll never put it on for you," he said.

Chuck's arms unfurled, and she plastered a sweet smile on her face.

"That's better." Sam levered himself off the floor and went to the closet, hanging the costume back in its proper place.

Charlotte let out a noise of protest. "Hey, you said you'd put it on!"

"I said that I would never put it on if you told my family. If I showed you now, what would stop you from running out and telling Carmen?"

"My honour?" she said, her voice hopeful.

Sam snorted. "Ha!"

"Fine, you're right." Charlotte threw her hands up in the air. "I'd tell her. I have no honour."

"Ah! And so you wait." Gently pushing her out of the way, Sam reached into the depths of the closet, digging around before pulling out a box. "Here's your slow cooker."

\*\*\*

"I've got to head to work." Sam set his napkin down on the table and used his finger to scavenge sauce from along the edge of his dish. "It doesn't feel right going to work after a meal like that. It's like... If I don't sit down and let my digestive tract enjoy it as much as my mouth did, I'm doing your cooking an injustice."

Charlotte grinned, pushing away from the table. "Since you're going off to heal and potentially save lives, the food and I will forgive you."

Sam groaned and rubbed his belly. "I think you give me much too much credit."

"And I think you give yourself too little." She stared into

his eyes for a moment, daring him to contradict her.

He broke the contact first and stood, picking up his plate. "I'll clean these up and get changed."

Charlotte grabbed the other before he could reach across the table for it. "You go change. I'll do this." She held out her hand, making a give-it-over motion with her fingers.

Sam scowled, refusing to relinquish the plate. "No way, my ma would have my head if I let you do the dishes after you cooked."

Charlotte growled, whirling away to take her dish to the sink. Then she turned to him, hands on her hips. "Sam, you're letting me stay here. You've been the most supportive person I could ever ask for through these last few days." Her voice roughened, and she swallowed. "I don't know what I would have done without you." She turned to the sink, starting the water. For a moment, she kept her back turned to him, drawing a deep breath that shook slightly. "I think that entitles me to spoil you a bit," she said after a second.

Sam took a step toward her. His arms ached to wrap around her, to protect her. The air seemed to thicken, and he wondered if Charlotte noticed. She must have sensed his gaze because she turned with her brow raised. "Are you okay?"

Sam shook his head, snapping himself from her spell. "Yeah," he said, clearing his throat sharply. "I'm great."

She gave him an odd look, then turned back to the dishes. Sam shoved his hands into his pockets, turned, and left the room.

Ten minutes later, dressed in scrubs and a hoodie, Sam came down from his room to find Chuck standing at the kitchen island with a sponge in her hand while she gazed around, a wistful look on her face. Leaning against the door frame, Sam watched her, perplexed. "Whatcha doin', Chuck?" he asked after a moment.

With a little shriek, she jumped and spun to face him, her cheeks flushing. "I was looking at it."

Sam cocked his head. "At what?"

"Your kitchen. Your beautiful, beautiful kitchen." She sighed, the sort of soft expulsion of air some women emit at the sight of shoes they couldn't afford.

Sam glanced around, then shrugged. He'd never thought about it too much. It was a good day when he had the time to make a sandwich before going into the living room and falling asleep on the couch. "Yeah, it's nice, I guess."

Charlotte cast him a withering glare. "It's literally my dream kitchen, and you're squandering it."

"I'm always gentle when I wipe the counters," he said, then ducked out the doorway to avoid the sponge she launched at his head.

"Bye, Chuck," he called as he pulled on his shoes, unable to wipe the grin off his face. "See you in the morning."

"Goodbye, Samuel," she called back in a sticky-sweet voice. "Have a lovely night, *dear.*"

# CHAPTER 13

Charlotte climbed the steps to Sam's loft bedroom with a sense of curious trepidation. He'd told her to come up and use the bathtub whenever she wanted, but it still felt as though she were intruding on Sam's personal territory. Pausing on the top level, she stared around at the room, mouth ajar.

"Well, of course, it's beautiful up here too," she muttered. Sam had left the blackout blinds open, and the inlaid ceiling windows allowed the grey winter light to poke dismally at the room. One wall was painted deep hunter green, and a few pieces of rough, rustic wood furniture gave the place a masculine beauty. She knew Sam would have carefully selected each for a reason. A side table she was sure Sawyer had crafted sat beside a perfectly made king-sized bed with a duvet resembling a cloud.

"What man lives like this?' she asked the empty room. Glancing around once more, she went into the bathroom.

The en-suite boasted a jetted tub. Charlotte stared at it for a full minute before she started pulling off her clothes. Cranking the knobs, she sat at the edge and then braided her hair while the water level climbed.

The heat sank its teeth into her aches and pains, making

her flinch and moan until it submerged her. As the knots eased and released their painful grip on her muscles, Charlotte dropped lower and lower in the tub until only her face peeked from the water.

Floating in the comfortable silence, she could nearly forget the press of reality lurking beyond the bathroom walls. She did her best to leave it at the edge of the porcelain and breathed in the steam, the lingering scent of sandalwood, while knot after knot released itself.

It would have been all too easy to stay that way for the rest of the day. But as the water chilled, the world crept back in. Charlotte sighed and sat up. With great deliberation, she closed her eyes and summoned every issue that plagued her one by one to the forefront.

Her father was healing slowly, but he was improving. The doctors were confident his health would continue to improve. There was no saying what the long-term damage would be yet. The doctors said there would be some, but they should be minimal with luck and healing. Memories of that night caused her heart to pound. Her throat thickened, and for a moment, she allowed herself to feel it all before she pushed it away.

Next was Charles. She liked him well enough but couldn't seem to get anywhere with him. She realized this was the first time she'd thought of him in days. He called once to check up when he received her tearful message upon arrival at the hospital, but she hadn't heard from him since. Curiously enough, his lack of attention scarcely bothered her, and she understood why. It all boiled down to Sam. Thoughts of Sam tainted her every interaction with Charles.

Sam.

Why had the spark that ignited between them at the wedding come as such an absolute shock to her? Things would never be the same between them, which scared her, but what if that was precisely what she needed to decide?

The water had turned frigid. Charlotte considered

adding hot water but then used her toes to pull out the plug with a sigh. Shivering, she wrapped herself in a towel, then used another to wring the water from her braid before wandering out of the bathroom.

One wall of Sam's room, from the slanting roof to floor was covered with shelving. Most held books and an array of pictures.

At least three shelves held *Archie* comics. She laughed to herself, pulling one down to run her fingers through the colourful pages. Growing up, Sam always had his face buried in a comic book or novel. On more days than she could count, Charlotte had walked with him after school to pick up the most recent issue of one thing or the other. They'd sit together on a bench at the park near the Stevensons' house and share a chocolate bar, their heads bent together as they read. She knew Sam had withstood a lot of flak from his friends for hanging out with her. She'd been hardly more than a kid when he was a teen, but they'd formed a strong bond.

Blinking away unexpected tears, she replaced the comic on the shelf. Goosebumps moved over her damp skin. Charlotte turned to retrieve her clothes when a picture caught her eye. It sat at the edge of one of the higher shelves in front of a collection of Tolkien novels in a simple wooden frame. Charlotte lifted it cautiously. It was her and Sam in their wedding finery, Carmen and Sawyer visible in the background, laughing. However, the bride and groom were blurred. The photographer had set Charlotte and Sam in their sights, though neither of them had known. Neither she nor Sam seemed aware the picture was being taken.

They had been dancing, she thought, and just stepped apart. Their bodies were still angled toward each other, her face upturned to Sam's. Whoever snapped the shot caught their faces at just the right angle, one light head, one dark, tipped close like the two kids who'd sat together in the park. Charlotte's eyes were almost closed, her smile flying wide with the type of laughter that only flowed when a person felt their most comfortable. Sam's gaze was on her face, his lips curved upward, displaying his single dimple. It was his eyes, though, the look in them, that caused her breath to catch and her heart to falter. He was drinking her in. Memorizing the story of her at that moment. A look she would expect to see shared between Sawyer and Carmen or Dan and Alice. A gaze so saturated with love and longing it was tangible even through the glossy paper.

Charlotte set the photo down with a thud and stepped backward, struggling to pull her eyes away from it.

# CHAPTER 14

"Chuck? You here?" Sam tossed his keys into the basket on the entryway table and bent to untie his shoes. "It smells great whatever you are doing!"

Nose in the air, sniffing like a bloodhound, he made his way to the kitchen. Charlotte stood at the stove, her back to him. When she didn't turn with her usual ready smile Sam frowned. "Chuck? Everything all right?"

Stepping up beside her, Sam laid a hand on her shoulder, glanced into the pot she stirred, and dipped his head, trying to see her face.

"I'm all right," she said finally, her voice strained.

"Don't lie to me," Sam said. "You're shaking." His heart speeding with anxiety, Sam grabbed her hand and extracted the spoon from it before turning her toward him. "Is your dad okay? Charlotte. You're scaring me."

Shaking her head, she pulled herself out of whatever daze she was in and blinked at him, then cleared her throat. "My dad is fine. I haven't heard anything else since this afternoon."

Sam released a breath he hadn't known he was holding. "Then what is going on?"

"I found the picture in your room."

Sam frowned. "Which picture? I have tons. Mom gives me more every year."

"You and I, at the wedding. I— What do you want from me, Sam?" She blurted the words as if holding them in her mouth would scald her tongue.

Sam let the hand drop from her shoulder, his gut squeezing. "What about that photo makes you ask me that? I don't understand why you're upset."

She gave him a look that showed she doubted his intelligence. "Answer me. Do you...do you want to be with me, Sam?"

"Maybe." He clenched his hands at his sides while his stomach launched itself into a free fall toward his feet. "Yes. It's been something I've considered over the years."

"Why did you never tell me?" Charlotte whispered.

"I suppose I was scared," he said. Terrified would have been more accurate.

Drawing a shaky breath, Charlotte took a step toward him, reaching to thread her fingers through his. "I think I want to try, too."

It was everything he'd wanted to hear for so very long, yet still, the niggling sensation of worry swirled in his gut.

"Not unless you're really in, Charlotte." He squeezed her fingers. "Maybe now isn't the right time to decide. You have a lot on your mind."

Charlotte stared down at their joined hands. "I want to be in, Sam."

He closed his eyes fleetingly, unable to look at her. "You want to? Or you are?"

"What's the diff—"

"There's a difference," he interrupted. The words bit out harsher than he intended.

Charlotte scowled at him. "Why are you so obstinate, Samuel?"

"You know me well enough to know if you want me or not, Charlotte?"

"I want you." Charlotte took a step closer. "I haven't

been able to get that night at the wedding out of my head."

Neither had Sam. His memory loved to torment him with flashing images. He woke with the feel of her soft skin, the roundness of her curves, tingling in his palms, only to find his bed empty.

"Chuck, I'm fucking terrified," he whispered.

Her dark eyes widened. "Why?" she asked. Her voice was wire taut. As if a world balanced on his answer.

Sam swallowed. Why had he said anything? The words that made sense moments ago now tumbled in his brain like rocks in a dryer. Loud and empty.

"Because I can't help but worry you might use me as a substitute for my brother."

The blood drained from Charlotte's face, leaving her caramel skin sallow. She stumbled back, her hips coming up against the counter. Hurt carved furrows across her brow.

"How could you say such a thing?" she whispered. Pain and fury flashed in her dark eyes.

"I know all about unrequited feelings." Sam's throat worked against the band of emotion hampering his breathing. "I've been suffering from them even longer than you. I know they don't just go away. What if you only think you want me?"

Charlotte lost the fight against the tears forming in her eyes. Sam knew at that moment what it was to have his heart break. He'd ruined everything. He stared at her fingertips. They floated in the chasm between them, unsure and glossed with the tears she used them to catch. Then she let them drop away.

"I don't understand." The confusion in her voice drove another wedge into Sam's heart. "I never even suspected until the wedding. Even that night, I thought we were lonely, caught in the spell. Then I saw that photo. And I talked to Carmen, and I find out you've been keeping this from me for so, so long. Why didn't you just tell me?" Her voice came out high and sharp, close to hysterical.

Sam's eyes slid closed. He was a coward. None of this

would have happened if he hadn't been such a fucking coward.

"I'm sorry, Chuck." The words ground in his throat, sharp as crushed glass. "I wanted... I was selfish."

"That's the kicker, Sam. You're the least selfish person I know." She shook her head. "Finish your sentence. Tell me what you wanted because I need to hear you say it."

"I don't—"

"Tell me, Sam!" Her voice cracked sharp as a slap.

Sam winced, his fists clenching at his sides to stop himself from grabbing her. "You! Always you, Charlotte. Every time I laid eyes on you since I was sixteen, you were a big-mouth kid who followed me around. But, goddamn it, when you weren't there, I looked for you and missed you so badly I ached." The words were punched out of him, weighted by years of restraint.

Charlotte closed her eyes, features contorted as though the weapon of his statement had inflicted physical damage. "All these years?" she asked. "I don't understand why you didn't just tell me. I can't wrap my head around this!"

She made it sound so simple. As if a confession of feelings would have led to some happy fairy-tale ending.

"I couldn't. Not with the way you looked at Sawyer. You pinned after him for years. How could I compete? I was older than you, weird and shy and..." Sam trailed off when he saw the flare of anger in Charlotte's eyes.

She took a hard step toward him. "What competition was there, Sam? Sawyer never wanted me. It was a crush. One I'm destined, apparently, to be blamed for, for the rest of my life."

The air left Sam's body in a rush. Had he been using Charlotte's feelings for Sawyer as an excuse? Blaming her all this time for something she had no control over?

"I never meant to hold it against you. I just... why would you go from wanting Sawyer to wanting me?"

He wasn't sure she would see it the way he did or entirely

understand. What he didn't expect was her stalking forward and driving her finger into his sternum, her face flushing an angry mottled red with fury.

"You listen to me, Sam Stevenson." She glowered up at him, small hands clenched at her sides as if at any moment she would pummel him. "I'm so sick of your *woe is me* shit. No one made you play second fiddle to your brother. That was all you." Her chest heaved with the force of her anger. Hair wild and eyes searing into his soul, she was the most sensational woman he'd ever laid eyes on.

"You are kind, and you are sweet," she continued, thumping her finger against his chest in emphasis of each point. "You have the most generous heart of anyone I've ever met, and God damn it, you're sexy, okay? Just because your little brother could give Thor a run for his money doesn't automatically make you an ogre! Stop being such a martyr." Her palms connected with his chest once. Twice. Not hard, but he stumbled back, more from the blow of her words than the physical touch.

"I'm sorry," he repeated. Charlotte growled and gave him another shove. It was odd, Sam thought as he stumbled again. All the times he'd witnessed Charlotte fly off the handle, it had never been him on the receiving end of her wrath.

"Stop saying sorry!" she yelled. "Stand up for yourself. Accept that you're amazing, for fuck's sake!" Her hands hit his chest again, and Sam caught them in his, gripping tight to keep her from hitting him again. Charlotte struggled against his grip for a moment, then the fight went out of her as suddenly as it had come. She deflated against his chest, and Sam wrapped his arms around her. Charlotte allowed him to hold her against him, cupping a hand around her head. Her breathing still came in rasping pulls, and Sam rested his chin against the top of her head. An errant curl tickled his nostril, but he didn't move.

"Thank you," he whispered against the rose-scented knot of her hair.

She twisted to glare up into his face. "Thank you?" she asked, her voice thick.

"For always standing by me, for calling me on my bullshit."

Her body relaxed against his slightly. "No one's ever thanked me for yelling at them before."

Sam gave her a weak smile. "I know it means you care."

She was silent for a moment, then sighed. "Things keep changing, Sam."

"I know, and they always will. The only constant, right?" Guilt kept its tenacious hold on him, sitting heavily on his heart. This change, the latest one, was his doing. Even now, the feel of her arms around his waist set his heart pounding. The blood rushed to parts oblivious to the seriousness of the situation. He shifted, putting an inch or two between them.

Charlotte sensed his restlessness and let her arms drop. "I should go." The fierceness of moments ago had passed. She was deflated. Exhausted. He tried to catch her gaze, but Charlotte refused to meet his eyes.

"Chuck—" he started.

She held up a hand, interrupting him. "I don't think we should spend any more time together tonight, Sam. I need...I don't know what I need. A time machine, perhaps."

"I'm sorry you regret it that much."

She glanced at him, dark brows dipping together. "Regret what?" she asked.

"What happened between us?"

Her face went flat, devoid of all the emotions that had burned there moments ago. "Is that what you think? That I've been wracked with regret over what happened between us?"

Sam nodded. "Isn't that why you're angry with me?"

Charlotte's sigh spoke of her level of frustration with him. "Sam, I don't regret you kissing me. I don't even regret nearly having sex with you."

Sam swallowed, heat tense in his gut at the words crossing her lips.

"What I regret is," she said with a sigh, "that you woke something in me I didn't know existed. You've been living with this for years. I haven't. But if you'd told me that night... maybe I wouldn't have spent three months trying to bury those feelings back down, those curiosities. Maybe I wouldn't have spent weeks trying to convince myself I was crazy for feeling the way I did afterward."

Sam couldn't find the words. Not the ones he needed to tell her what an idiot he had been. Not the ones that would make any of this better.

"I didn't know what to say," he whispered.

"You never even called," Charlotte said. "I thought I was just a hookup, and when it didn't work out, it was no skin off your back." She shook her head. "I thought it was only me that things changed for."

"I dialed your number or started a text to you every day," Sam said. He took a step toward her, needing to reassure her it was real for him.

"Then why didn't you?" She stared at him. "Why didn't you just call me?"

"I didn't know what you'd do. I thought you'd be angry. Or worse, you'd laugh and make a joke of that night. Part of me felt I'd taken advantage of you."

"I'm a grown woman, Sam. If I didn't want to kiss you, I would have said no. I wasn't so drunk that you need to feel guilty about that."

"I blew my chance at something I've wanted for seventeen years." It wasn't a question, and he didn't wish for or expect an answer from her.

Charlotte shoved her hands into her hair, yanking a few strands from the precarious top knot. "I don't know. I literally know nothing right now. My dad is still in the hospital, and there's Charles, who I like, and who likes me. He doesn't look for excuses not to be with me. I just don't *know* anymore."

There was a current beneath the words she spoke. A depth of layers she'd left unvoiced. Sam sensed each one as if she'd said them. Charles pursued her, hadn't allowed fear to dictate his actions. Sam stood still, his hope slipping through his fingers like grains of dry sand.

Charlotte's phone blared to life, making them both jump. For a moment, Sam thought she wouldn't answer. She stared into his face as if she didn't hear it, then she shook her head. After taking the phone from her pocket, she swiped the screen.

"Hey," she said. "Yes, we're still on. I'm just leaving my friend's place." She was quiet for a moment, meeting Sam's gaze one last time, then she turned away, walking to the door. "No, I'm fine. See you soon."

# CHAPTER 15

Charles met Charlotte a block from Sam's apartment building. She slid into the seat, and he twisted in his seat toward her. His cologne was floral and cloying. He pressed a quick kiss to her cheek and then settled back behind the wheel. "We don't have to do this," he said. "You look exhausted."

Charlotte struggled back against an overwhelming urge to snap at him. It was the first time he had been around since they admitted her father. How did he expect her to look?

"I'm actually not feeling great. Can we just get take-out and eat at your place?"

Charles's eyes creased with sympathy. He nodded and picked up her hand, massaging the spaces between her fingers. "Sounds good, quiet night and a movie? Do you have your stuff? You can stay and be closer to your dad."

So, he did realize her dad was sick. "All right." She couldn't go back to Sam's, and driving the forty-five minutes home alone was more than she could think about at the moment. "But I'll sleep on the couch. I'm just not ready for—" She waved a hand in the air between them.

Charles shook his head. Lifting her hand, he brushed his

lips across her knuckle. "No, of course not. Don't worry about that. I expect nothing. I just want you to get some rest."

***

When they were settled on Charles's couch with fragrant glasses of Merlot and steaming plates of Chinese take-out in front of them, Charlotte forced herself to relax.

"I'm sorry I wasn't here for you more this week," Charles said after the silence grew heavy.

"You're a busy man. I understand." The assurance relaxed a fraction of the petty resentment that continued to fester.

"I shouldn't have been so busy that I couldn't be there when you needed me."

"I'm fine. My dad will be fine. There was no need to disrupt your life as well."

Charles ate in silence for a few more moments. Charlotte pushed her food with the tines of her fork, leaving whorls of grease and sauce. She couldn't shake the image of Sam's face before she walked away. Was she destined to keep hurting him, even against her will? It was the last thing in the world she wanted.

"Tell me about your friend, Sam," Charles said in an unsettling moment of mind-reading. "You said she's a nurse?"

"Sam?" Charlotte looked up, blinking in surprise. "She?"

"Sam, the girl you were staying with?"

"Yes, I know. Sorry, I was thinking about something." Charlotte shook her head, trying to tamp down her rampaging thoughts. "Sam's great. I've known him since I was a kid. He was working the night they brought my dad in." She took a bite to avoid talking, and as an act of defiance to the past that kept stealing her focus.

Charles gave her an odd look, laying his fork on the edge

of his plate. "Sam's a guy?"

"Yeah."

Charles frowned. "So, not a Samantha."

"Sam as in Samuel. Samuel Sterling Stevenson, to be exact. His parents have a weird obsession with S names."

"You know his middle name?"

Charlotte closed her eyes, seeking patience. She wasn't sure she could endure petty jealousy on top of everything else at the moment. "I've known him for twenty years, Charles. We saw each other every day when we were kids. You learn a thing or two about a person over that amount of time."

"Have you guys ever... you know. Dated?" He avoided her eyes when he asked, proving Charlotte's suspicions that it wasn't dating he was asking about.

Charlotte set her plate on the coffee table with a thud. Her mind tossed random flashes at her. Sam's lips brushing over her jaw. His fingers furrowing into her hair. The rasp of his palms over his skin. As she struggled with her temper, her body heated at the memory of what passed between her and Sam. The weight of his hands over her bare skin. The sweet whiskey-scented curve of his mouth intoxicating her.

"No, we have not, though that is absolutely none of your business."

A flush darkened Charles's face. He twisted toward her on the couch. "Sorry if I am not comfortable with my girlfriend hiding the fact she's been staying at another guy's place for the last week."

Charlotte's tentative hold on her temper snapped. Blood tingled in her fingertips and moved in a rush through her veins. Slowly, she rose off the couch, fists clenched so tight her nearly nonexistent fingernails dug crescents into her palms. Her face felt numb.

"I don't even know what part of that ignorant, chauvinistic, sexist statement to tear to shreds first." Charlotte stepped closer to where Charles sat and brandished a finger at his face. "Even if we'd talked about being exclusive, which we have not, slapping the label 'girlfriend' on me doesn't give you any right to dictate who I spend my time with." She sucked in a deep breath, and when Charles opened his mouth, she rushed on. "I know perfectly well why you assumed Sam was a woman, and I'd like to inform you it's the twenty-first century. Get your head out of your ass. You'd be damned lucky to have Sam Stevenson as your nurse."

"I never implied he wasn't a good nurse." Charles was on his feet now. He had little height on her, but the inches he did, he used to his advantage. Pushing his chest out like a bull, staring down his face at her. "Why are you acting so crazy? Are you bipolar or some shit?"

Charlotte froze. She was dizzy with anger. Now another emotion spread through her. "Don't say that," she whispered. "I've every sane right to be angry at you. Typical. A woman gets mad over being treated in a shit way, and she's the crazy one." Her face alternated between hot and numb, tremors making her fingers twitch at her sides. "I need to go."

Charles sighed and sank down onto the couch, pushing both hands through his perfectly gelled hair until it stood on end. It was the first time Charlotte had seen him disheveled.

"Chuck, come on, let's have a drink and talk."

"Don't call me Chuck," she spat.

He glowered at her. Charlotte glared right back. She was not about to be cowed by him.

"Fine." His lips took an ugly twist, and seizing his wine glass, he slammed back the rest of the liquid in one swallow. "Do whatever you want."

Charlotte stared at him for a long moment, trying to feel something through her anger, regret, and guilt. Nothing surfaced past the burn of fury. Nothing but the aching knowledge this man was not Sam. He would never be Sam, and she was done here. Without another word, Charlotte picked up her jacket and left.

\*\*\*

Charlotte was nearly outside of the city when the tears hit her. They welled up out of nowhere, closing her throat and streaming down her face until it was impossible to see the road. With shaking hands, Charlotte guided the car to the side of the highway and slammed the gearshift into park.

Then she sat, crying in the way a person could only do when they were alone. Ugly, snotty, and unhindered. Naked. The tears were not for Charles but for the disappointed pain of another mistake. However, most came from a place more profound where all the hidden fears and trapped emotions waited to spring forth and ambush her. The past week, she'd pretended she hadn't nearly lost the only family she had left. She had been stable for her dad, and when she found she couldn't be, Sam had been there, familiar and loving. Now he was sitting hurt and alone because of her.

Charlotte sensed the dark waters lapping at her ankles. Despair was too deadly a road to tread. It would swallow her if she let it. Stark loneliness engulfed her, pulling her down.

How much worse had it been for her mother before the end? She'd been trapped in a country where she barely spoke the language, struggling with only a baby for company day in and day out.

Charlotte gulped a breath. Filled her lungs to capacity and released it, did it again and then again. She used the sleeve of her jacket to mop the rivulets of tears off her face and, for lack of a better option, her scarf to blow her nose. Air still came shakily to her lungs. She felt steadier aside from the sick pounding of her head from crying. She was less ready to burst apart at the seams. Leaning her head against the steering wheel, she lifted her phone and pressed the tiny icon of a serious face.

"Chuck?" The answer came on the first ring.

"Sam?" Her voice broke, though she fought to keep it steady. "Can I come back to your place?"

# CHAPTER 16

He met her on the stairs up to his apartment. Sam knew the second he answered the phone that she needed him. Perhaps that was his lot in life. To be the one who always caught her. The one she ran to. Would it be enough? The aching response of his body when he scooped her against his chest told him it was not. If it came to this or nothing? Was he strong enough to endure? He knew he would have to be. What else could he do?

Charlotte did not speak, and he did not ask her to. She walked up and placed her face to his chest, sliding her arms around his waist. She was shaking, and a salty, lingering scent gave away the secret of her tears. It felt as natural as breathing to lift her against his chest and take her inside.

Sam set her down at the door, bending to remove her boots. She lifted each foot like a child, allowing him to slip them off. After Charlotte was free of her jacket, Sam hung it on the hook. Then he took her hand, leading her down the hall to the stairs, up to his bedroom. She said nothing, silent and still beside the tremors that wracked her limbs. If ever for a second she doubted his intentions, it never showed. Her tear-swollen eyes were half-closed as if she could not stand to keep them open.

Sam pulled back the quilt on his bed and tugged her over. When she crawled inside, he tucked the blankets tight around her and switched off the lamp. Taking his pillow, he turned.

"Where are you going?" Her voice was rough.

Sam paused. "Downstairs to sleep on the couch."

"Stay with me, please," she whispered. The words floated to Sam through the darkened room.

He should say no, but the loneliness in her voice drove a spike into his heart. He nodded and eased under the blankets at her side, cocooning them both in the cloud against the chill.

Sliding one hand under her knees, he folded her up against his warmth. The palm of his free hand stroked her tangled hair until the shaking in her limbs subsided. She fell into sleep like a stone in a pond, instantly submerged. It didn't matter to Sam that she hadn't spoken besides that simple plea. He had never needed words to understand Charlotte. Lying engulfed in her smell, the warmth of her body against his, Sam drifted back to sleep.

***

When Sam blinked awake, a grey shrouded sun hung like a stubborn balloon outside the window. He lay still, disoriented by the comfort of Charlotte tucked tight against him. For someone who had never understood the appeal of lying in bed late into the morning, Sam knew he would be content to stay there for hours. The muscles in his back ached, but he ignored them. If he moved, Charlotte may stir and feel the evidence of how much he enjoyed waking to her ass pressed against him.

Charlotte, with her knack for timing, chose that moment to yawn and stretch. Like a cat, she arched her body backward, pressing her ass right into his raging hard-on. A moan escaped Sam before he could stop it. His face heated and, though he hadn't thought it possible, he grew harder.

Charlotte stilled, the shuddery jerk of her gasp bouncing around the silent bedroom. Then, tentatively, she pressed back into him again.

Sam put a hand on her hip, unsure if he meant to stop her or pull her tighter to him. A shiver ran through Charlotte and made the twirls of hair clinging to his pillow shudder. The bone of her hip curved under his fingers, her t-shirt hiked up so the tips rested against her taut skin. He would only have to slide his hand forward... Sam stopped the thought in its tracks. Neither of them moved. They lay halted, sensibilities battling with needy bodies. Charlotte wanted him. At that moment, Sam didn't doubt the fact. Her body hummed beneath his touch, and the chilled air in his bedroom was thick with the musk of sleep and desire.

He could lay still no longer. Good sense and morals could only prevail for so long. He moved, and it should have been away from Charlotte. It should have been off the bed and out of the room. He should do something, think about anything else to ease the incessant ache. Instead, he spread his hand open across the gentle curve of her abdomen. Pressed her back and upward until his erection lodged so tight against her ass, he saw stars.

Charlotte whimpered, her head lolling back on the pillow, exposing her throat to his searching lips. Beneath the caramel of her skin, her jugular pulsed. Sam groaned and dipped his head forward, dragging his teeth over that pulsing evidence of her desire. Pressed his mouth to the fluttering throb just beneath the surface of her sweet skin. Her hips bucked, and she hissed in a breath. Sam's world narrowed to only Charlotte, the heat of their bodies between the blankets that shielded them and the desperate need clawing through his abdomen.

Placing her hand atop Sam's, Charlotte guided his fingers lower, a moan moving through her chest when he reached the juncture of her thighs.

"Lord, Charlotte." Sam's voice was rough as gravel. "I want you."

"Please." The word came out as a sob, and she pressed into his exploring fingers. His touch slipped over the slickness of her folds as he searched out and discovered the tiny knot hiding there.

"Oh." It was half-word, half-purr, signalling his success in finding what he sought. Sam used his thumb and pointer to pluck at her. She arched, moaning as she thrust her hips against his hand. Her ass rubbed the length of Sam's aching cock, and he squeezed his eyes shut, fighting the urge to come right there.

Without warning, Charlotte rolled, pinning his body beneath her. He could feel the wet heat of her through the cotton pajama pants he regrettably still wore. "Oh, please, no sudden movements," he groaned. "I'm scared I'll embarrass myself."

Charlotte answered by leaning forward to slide her lips across his. At the same time, she rubbed herself against his hard length. Her nipples were hard as pebbles against his chest, and Sam's mouth watered with the need to taste them. He grabbed her hips and stilled her. "Stop," he rasped. "I don't want this to end with me in wet pants like an adolescent. I want you so bad, Chuck."

"Please, tell me"—she sat back, staring down at him through the dark curtain of her hair—"that you have a condom this time."

All Sam could do was nod toward the bedside table. Charlotte leaned over. He seized her thighs to steady her and to anchor himself as he fought for control. As Charlotte fumbled with the box, his cell buzzed on the table. Charlotte glanced down at the phone, then frowned, going still.

"Ignore it." Sam seized a handful of her ass and squeezed to augment his argument. Charlotte ignored him and picked up the phone.

"Sam," she said, her voice strained.

"Yes?"

"Who is Jane and why is she, quote 'coming commando to your date tonight?'"

"Shit." Sam groaned and rubbed a trembling hand over his face.

"Do you have a girlfriend?" she whispered, her brown eyes huge.

"No, I've only gone out with her twice," Sam said, shaking his head and fighting to think over the pounding of his heart and the angry protests of his cock.

"Enough times, apparently, for her to feel comfortable enough to leave her panties at home."

"Charlotte."

"You're here, doing this to me, last night, telling me all the things you told me… And you have a woman waiting for you?" Tears filled her eyes, but she didn't look away. "You were supposed to be one of the good ones, Sam."

"It's not like that." Sam reached a hand to her cheek, but Charlotte jerked away.

"Oh, God." She rolled off him and onto her feet, adjusting her clothing. "I don't know. I don't know what to think about anything. Every time I turn around, there is something new hiding behind the fucking corner."

As if to illustrate the point, her cell phone sprang to life. Closing her eyes for a moment, Charlotte turned and fished it out of her jeans pocket.

"It's the hospital." She raised it to her ear. "Hello?"

Sam tried to hear but could make out nothing more than a tiny squeak from the other end.

Charlotte nodded. "Yes, I see. That sounds good. Thank you so much, Doctor Burke."

Sam winced at the name, shame burning hot as acid in his chest.

She hung up the phone and stared down at it. "I've got to go. They are releasing my dad."

Sam sat up. "Do you want me to come with you?"

"No, I think… I think I need space from you, Sam. I've got to get Dad settled. They want to give him a home nurse for the next bit, and I have to pick up things for the house to help him be comfortable. I just…I need to clear my head."

"Charlotte, please text me if you need help with anything. I'm serious." Sam caught her eyes and refused to let her look away. "I love your dad like my own. I want to know how he's doing."

The tear welled in her eyes, and she turned from him, nodding. "I know."

"Chuck." He stopped her again as she was about to leave the room.

"Yeah?"

"Jane, she's my... she's my Charles. She's that attempt at *something*, you know?"

She stopped, half in the room, halfway out, but nodded again. "I'll do some thinking, Sam. I promise. Once this all settles down."

Sam swallowed hard. He desperately wanted to grab her, beg her to let him come with her to the hospital. She shouldn't have to do this alone. However, he knew the depths of her stubbornness and knew that he had hurt her again.

"Bye, Chuck," he said. He wasn't sure if she heard him. The front door closed a minute later, and Sam sank back on his bed, both palms pressed to his forehead.

# CHAPTER 17

Sam was two blocks from the hospital when his phone buzzed in his pocket. He pulled it out, his heart jumping with hope. It had done that every time he received a message for the last two weeks. Ever since he had last seen Chuck. So far, he'd only experienced disappointment, but his heart refused to give up its hopeful vigil.

The screen displayed a text message from his father. Swallowing disappointment, Sam swiped the notification open. *I'm in town and near the hospital. Grab a coffee before your shift?*

Sam blinked and reread the message before typing his reply. *Meet you in the waiting room in 15 minutes?*

His steps sped up. He would throw his things in his locker and have plenty of time to prepare for his shift. He usually arrived early Saturdays to give the lady at the charity shop a hand.

Lost in thought, Sam found himself at the hospital in no time. Sam made his way toward the front waiting room, pulling a sweatshirt over his scrubs and tucking his lanyard into his pocket.

It was half full. A man, his face grizzled by a life lived too hard, sat with a blond boy in an oversized jacket. As

Sam passed, the boy glanced up, then away. Three chairs down, a muscle-bound twenty-something sat with a blood-soaked rag clutched to his face. A hockey bag bulged by his feet, a stick protruding from the busted zipper like an errant limb.

The hockey tournament. Every year it brought the hospital staff a wide assortment of bloody noses, concussions, and the occasional heart attack. Plenty of middle-aged men viewed the weekend-long tourney as their yearly claim to manly retribution and physical exertion. The entire scene had the makings of a long night. Sam checked his phone. Five minutes and his dad would look for him.

The little boy was alone now, head hanging as he studied something in his lap. Sam went to walk by, then, on impulse, approached him.

"Hey buddy, whatcha got there?" he asked.

The boy scuttled back into the shelter of the seat's plastic embrace at the sound of Sam's voice. Huge brown eyes flicked up to Sam's, then darted around the room. Sam squatted in front of the chair, bringing himself to the child's level.

"It's my Spider-Man." The voice was timid but steady.

"Awesome!" Sam grinned, careful to remain still. "I was always a Batman guy myself, but Spider-Man is really cool."

A shy smile curved the boy's lips. "I like Batman, but I don't have any other toys."

"Well, that's smart," Sam said. "You wouldn't want to bring too many here or you might lose them. Good to just have your favourite."

The boy studied Sam's face for a moment, then looked down at the toy. "I don't have any others at home either."

Sam's heart twisted. It was an old familiar ache. He could not be sure, but he guessed the boy was about seven. A similar age to his niece, who was loud and robust, with a room bursting with more toys than she knew what to do with.

"Can I see him?" Sam asked. "Promise I'll be gentle."

Bottomless dark eyes roamed around once more. They remained on Sam's face longer this time and reminded him fleetingly of Chuck's. Eyes deep enough you could tumble right into them.

"Okay." The boy passed the toy to him. Most of the paint had worn away, and one hand looked as if it had been none too cleanly amputated by the jaws of a canine.

"Do you have a dog at home?" Sam asked. "I love dogs."

The blond head shook back and forth. "No, I found it like this. I think it got throwed away."

"Sweet," Sam said, turning the figure over in his hands once more before he passed it back. "Well, I think it makes Spider-Man look even tougher." When the boy reached out, Sam glanced down. The skinny wrist that protruded from the jacket sleeves was ringed in deep blue. Stark morbid bangles against pale, fresh skin. Sam swallowed the wave of angry nausea swelling in his throat.

"What happened there?" He forced his voice into a semblance of casual as he gestured toward the marks. Quick as gophers, the wrists disappeared back into their cuffs.

"No...nothing." Panic flared and burned in the brown eyes.

"Hey! What the hell you doin'?" a rough voice barked.

Sam pressed the toy firmly back into the small hands and rose to his feet. "Good after—" He didn't have time to finish. The man stomped toward Sam, lips knotted in a fury, deep-set eyes wild. Without pausing, he snatched the hockey stick from the bloodied hockey player's bag as he passed.

"Hey now!" Sam spread his hands at his sides but planted his feet, watching the wooden blade. "I was just talking to your boy, saying hi. I work here."

"Don't *hey* me! I know what you're up to. Trying to take my kid away from me. Just trying to get some meds for my back, and you vultures swoop in. I got news for you. You're not getting him."

The scabbed face twisted into a snarl, and he stabbed the blade toward Sam's stomach. Sam reacted, turning his body sideways, but the man was faster than he expected. The flat edge drove into his side and propelled the air out of his lungs in an agonizing whoosh. Mouth wide, Sam tipped forward in a breathless attempt to move away. The stick caught him across the jaw, and fireworks burst in a giddy buzz behind his lids, saturating his oxygen-deprived brain with dizzying light.

How stereotypical, his frantic mind supplied with cynical timing, as the darkness tickled at the edges of his consciousness. A proper Canadian beating. He hit the floor hard, twisting to guard his organs and head as the stick drove into the floor inches from his face with a *crack*.

A boot connected with his back, and then nothing else mattered but the stomach-twisting crunch that echoed through his body. The sound mingled with the screams of other patients, the shouts of medical staff. Pain flared white-hot as Sam gasped for air. Iron bloomed on his tongue as his chin connected with the floor.

The last thing that made sense in the face of the impending darkness was the bellow of his father's voice over the din.

*\*\*\**

Sawyer was sound asleep, his limbs tangled with Carmen's when the cell phone on the bedside table blared to life. Strains of "Lean on Me" sprang around their bedroom. With a growl, Sawyer rolled, fumbling for the phone. Carmen had switched the ringtone for when his dad called, and he still couldn't figure out how to change it back.

"You're fixing that in the morning," he rasped at his wife, who sprawled in oblivion at his side. "Hello?"

"Sawyer, it's your father."

"Yeah, Dad, I know. What's going on? It's like—" He squinted at the clock. It read 11:30. Sawyer groaned and rubbed a hand over his face. "God, what happened to me?"

"You got married," came Carmen's sleepy mumble from

the other side of the bed.

"Sawyer, for fuck's sake, listen to me." His dad's deep voice was loud and strained over the phone. The hairs on Sawyer's arms rose.

"It's your brother. He's about to go into surgery.

Sawyer shot upright. "What the hell! Is he okay? What happened?"

"Some maniac in the ER snapped and beat him up." Dan drew a breath. Sawyer could hear it shudder. "His lung, it's… it's punctured. They have to re-inflate it somehow. Like my son is a fucking balloon—" Dan's words ground to a halt.

Sawyer could hear him breathing through his nose and out through his mouth. Alice's trick. She always sat them down and made them breathe that way when they were kids and needed a moment to calm down.

"I'm on my way," Sawyer said, jumping up and going to dig through a dresser for a pair of jeans.

"We," Carmen corrected. She was beside him in an instant, her long pale limbs flashing in the dark as she began pulling on clothes. "Do we need to pick up Alice?"

"Yes." Dan and Sawyer spoke at the same time.

"Call Chuck," Carmen ordered as she clasped her bra. "Tell her we will be there in ten minutes."

Sawyer frowned, hopping into his jeans. His hands were shaking so badly it took him three tries to get the button done. "Why do we need to wake Charlotte up?"

Carmen shot him a look that said she would lecture him on his stupidity later. "Trust me and call her."

L.E. WAGENSVELD

# CHAPTER 18

Sam's head hurt. He groaned, and the sound hurt his throat. Distorted fragments of memories flickered through his muddied brain as he blinked at the white ceiling. There was a rustle beside him, a sleepy murmur, and then Charlotte's face, hazy, as she peered down at him.

"Sam?" she whispered. "Are you all right?"

Sam squinted up at her, struggling to bring her into focus. "Chuck?" The light behind her head made her glow like an angel. "What the hell happened?"

Tears brimmed and ran over her cheeks, dropping to create dark spots on the blue fabric of his hospital gown.

Charlotte pressed her fingertips to her mouth and let out a long, shaky sigh. "You scared the shit out of us, Sam."

"What happened?" he repeated. Charlotte didn't answer. A high, rushing sob escaped her, and she grasped his chin in her hands, kissing him hard on the lips. She leaned her forehead against his, her breath shuddering across his aching skin.

"Some maniac attacked you with a hockey stick. He hit you in the back and in the face." Her voice broke, and Charlotte paused. Her hands dipped lower to rasp across the roughness of bandages. Below them, his skin was sore and tight. Drawn together. He recognized the sensation of stitches through his flesh.

"I heard something break when he kicked me." He could remember that much, then things went hazy. "What was it?"

Charlotte let out a choked noise and turned her face away from him for a second. "Your rib," she said after a moment. "It punctured your lung, and they rushed you into surgery. Your dad was there. He nearly got himself arrested."

"Dad was there?"

Charlotte nodded. "Security had to pull him off the guy. They held them both until the cops got there. They took Dan in, but he was so frantic to get back here that they let him go. That's when he called Sawyer."

Faint memories of being surprised by his dad's text message. The roar of Dan's voice over the chaos in the waiting room. "There was a kid," Sam said, squeezing his eyes shut. That was how it had all happened. A little boy.

"They called social services, I think," Charlotte said. "We can find out later about that. You need to rest now."

Sam nodded, then regretted it immediately. "Okay. Hit that red button for me, will you, Chuck?"

Charlotte's lips curled up a fraction as she reached across him to push the red call button. Her finger had scarcely lifted when the curly head of a nurse popped through the door.

"You all right there, Sammy?" She smiled down at him, but the etching of concern around her eyes betrayed her.

"Yeah, thanks, Val." Sam tried to push himself up, then eased back onto the pillows when the room spun. "Can I have more of the good stuff yet?"

"You bet," she said, bobbing her head with a wink.

"So?"

Val looked down at him, her lips tightening as she shook her head, then busied herself checking his chart. "Leave it to you, Sammy. Traumatic pneumothorax from steel toes to the ribs. Six stitches to the laceration on your face from the blade of a hockey stick. Are you trying to prove you're Canadian? We all knew already; we figured it out when you were so damn nice all the time."

Sam let out a pained snort, and the two of them sat in silence while Val bustled about the room. When she finished, she came to the bed and gave Sam's hand a squeeze. "Call if you need anything, you hear me?"

"Yes, ma'am."

Then she was gone as quickly as she'd appeared.

"Val was born in Washington," Sam said.

"That explains the Canadian jokes," Charlotte said, settling herself down into the chair once more.

"Chuck," Sam said. It was a struggle to get the words out. The painkillers were already flickering through his veins, lapping up the pain it encountered until he was numb. "You don't have to stay," he mumbled. With a considerable effort, he turned his head on the pillows so he could see Charlotte where she hovered at the edge of his bed.

"I know that. But I will stay," Charlotte said. There was a tilt to her chin that told him arguing would do him no good. He didn't have the energy for it, anyway.

"You're beautiful," he said instead, his voice slurred.

"Those drugs are making you crazy." Colour washed over her cheeks, and she reached out, running one finger along the back of his hand where it lay on the bedsheet. Sam turned his palm upward, capturing her fingers with his.

"Thanks," she whispered. "You're not so bad yourself when you're not stitched up like Frankenstein's monster."

Sam chuckled, then groaned at the spear of pain that shot through his back. "Is my dad still around?"

"Yes," Charlotte said. "Everyone is. We've been taking shifts sitting with you. Everyone else is asleep in the waiting room."

"Everyone? Who? Why?" He squinted at her. The effort to keep his eyes open was almost more than he could exert.

"What do you mean, why? Because we love you, idiot.

Carmen and Sawyer, your mom and dad. Sash is on her way; she had to wait for Pete to get home and stay with the kids."

"Oh, man," Sam groaned. "You guys didn't have to do that. It's not a big deal."

"No, Sam, you almost dying isn't a big deal to any of us." She glared at him. He was too euphoric with sedation and the pleasure of the realization of just how worried she was to let her anger bother him.

"I've never seen Dan this upset," she said, sinking back into the chair. She swallowed and tightened her fingers around his. "He said your lips were blue, and you were gasping and... and blood—" She waved a hand at her mouth. "Fuck, I'm happy you were in a hospital."

"Potty mouth," Sam mumbled.

Charlotte shook her head but couldn't hide the hint of a smile that played at the corners of her lips. "I'm not sure how you can joke."

"You either laugh or you cry." He tried to smile, but inexplicably, he felt more like crying instead. Morphine did that to him. Brought long-hidden emotions roiling to the surface for no particular reason. Charlotte's face was swimming before his eyes. The flickering images were back, dancing around his head. Weird, random, distorted fragments. Mr. Edwards, the smiling face of his dog grinning from a phone screen, Sam's parents.

"I lost Sasha's hamster," he blurted.

"Umm, sorry, what?" One of Charlotte's dark brows rose.

"I was nine, and Sasha was seven. I said I didn't want a hamster. Because if my parents weren't getting me a dog, I didn't want any other pet. Then I got home early one day, and Sash was at a dance." Sam shook his head. The scrape of his hair against the pillowcase made him wince. "The stupid thing was adorable, and I wished I hadn't been so stubborn. I took it out in the sunshine and made a little nest for it in the grass."

"Oh, no," Charlotte whispered.

"The phone rang. I figured it would be fine. I mean, why would you run away from a cozy home and two meals a day?"

"What did Sasha do when you told her?" Charlotte leaned closer, studying him with wide eyes.

"I didn't tell her. I left the cage door open just a tiny bit, ran to Noah's house, and hid. All these years, she thought she was the one who forgot to close the door."

Sam risked a look at her, ready to see the judgment on her face. Instead, her lips pressed tight, and her eyes sparkled with something that looked suspiciously like laughter.

"Oh, Sam." Charlotte shook her head. Her free hand floated up, hesitated, then stroked his hair back from his face. Her fingers were cool, the touch so soft that Sam's eyes drifted closed.

"I want a dog," he murmured.

She blinked, shaking her head in confusion. "I missed the random pet confessions memo for this evening's entertainment."

Sam sighed, turning his face into her touch. "Sorry. I'm hardly sure what I'm saying anymore."

"Why don't you get one?" Charlotte asked.

"Can't. How could I leave Archie alone all day while I work?"

"Archie?" she asked with a hint of amusement in her voice. Amusement and something else… pity?—he didn't want that.

"I can't get a dog," he groaned. "There's something I have to do."

"No, there is nothing you have to do besides heal," Charlotte scolded.

"I do. I have to… I have to… Mr. Edwards's dog. He has to say goodbye soon," Sam mumbled. That was it, what he'd been trying to remember.

"Sam, I don't know what you're talking about." Her fingers stopped moving and fell away. He ached to have them back.

"Just rest now," she murmured.

Opening his eyes, Sam tried to sit up, but Charlotte's hand on his chest stopped him, pressed him back into the sterile embrace of the hospital bed. "You need to relax; the drugs are making you loopy," she said, her voice stern.

"Mr. Edwards told me he wouldn't get to say goodbye to his dog." Hot liquid leaked from the corners of his eyes and over his cheeks. He wanted—he didn't know what he wanted. The bright hospital room was fading at the edges. A vignette was waiting to swallow the entire scene. He hissed through his teeth, desperate not to let it go. Not the moment, not the memory of what it was he needed to do. What if the next time he woke up, she wasn't there?

"Chuck?" He reached out to her. The tips of her fingers found his brow. Distracting him. Rubbing in small circles at his temples until her touch was all that mattered. He allowed his eyelids to slide closed.

"Chuck?" he mumbled again.

"Hush, sleep." She used her shirt sleeve to wipe his cheeks and drew her finger repeatedly down his nose. "Please rest," she whispered. The fingers came back to his hair, and Sam sighed in relief. Quietly, Charlotte began to sing. Some sweet, lilting tune in a familiar but still foreign language, especially to his muddled brain.

"Didn't know you spoke Spanish," he slurred.

"Some," Charlotte whispered, breaking her song. "It's a lullaby my mom used to sing to me. My dad memorized it. After she died, he sang it to me every night until I was probably much too old."

"Keep singing, please." Sam drifted off to images of Charlotte and the sensation of her lips warm on his cheek above the bandages.

\*\*\*

"I want to go home." Sam heard the sullenness in his

voice but couldn't bring himself to care. Deena paused in her whirl of tasks and turned a gimleted eye on him.

"Your parents are going to be here any moment, and they are taking you to their house. We decided going up and down all those stairs at your place isn't a good idea for a week or so."

Sam scowled. "Oh, you guys decided, did you?"

Deena matched him scowl for scowl. "Yes, and we are well aware of your thoughts on the matter. There is no need to voice them. We do not care."

"What would I do without all of you to make my decisions for me?" He flexed his hands on top of the sheets. He was being insolent and downright grumpy. The helplessness of his lung capacity and hindered movements infuriated him. Being trapped in the hospital bed made his skin crawl with frustration.

"You'd probably go home and rot in your own filth because you're too damned stubborn to allow anyone to help you." Deena shoved a pair of pants into his duffel bag, then turned back to him, one brow raised in challenge.

"I can move." Struggling, Sam raised himself a few inches toward a sitting position. Pain bloomed through his rips, and his lungs burned. "Fuck it. Fine," he growled. "I need help, but only for a few days!"

Deena made a humph in agreement and turned her back on him, busying herself with his chart.

Sam let her work for a few more moments in silence. "Hey, D?"

She turned to him, face wary. "Yes?"

Sam extended his hand toward his friend. "Thank you."

She took his hand but refused to meet his eyes for a moment. "Anytime," she said finally. "Now, let's get ready to busy you out of here." With a squeeze of his fingers, she released him and turned away. Sam didn't miss the deep breath or the rigid set of her shoulders.

.

# CHAPTER 19

"Hey, sweetie!" Alice greeted Charlotte with a hug when she reached the bottom of the stairs. "Thanks for coming. Hopefully, you can cheer him up because none of us can," she added in a whisper.

"He's feeling that good, hey?" Charlotte gave Alice a wry look, then turned her attention to Sam. "Hey, Stevenson," she said in an overly bright voice. "How are you feeling?"

He slumped on the couch, looking like he had spent the last few days sucking on lemons.

"Oh, you know, fantastic," he grumbled. "When you're thirty-four and your mother has to help you in the bathroom, life is all unicorns and rainbows."

Charlotte leaned toward Alice without taking her eyes off Sam. "So, he's in a good mood this morning?" she asked in a faux whisper. This time, Sam aimed his glare in her direction.

"It's nothing you don't do every day for others. What's wrong with us taking care of you?" Alice made to fluff the pillow behind his head, but Sam literally growled at her.

"I can take care of myself."

Charlotte fought the urge to smack him upside the head and settled on brandishing a finger at him. "Be nice to your mother," she warned.

Alice seemed unperturbed by either of them. "Fine, be a Grumpy Gus. I'm going to make you guys some cookies." She bustled out of the room. Charlotte eased down beside Sam, struggling to contain her laughter.

"What are you watching?" she asked after a few moments of silence.

For a second, she thought he wouldn't answer, then he said, "*Due South.*"

"I thought so! We used to watch this all the time, remember?"

"Yes."

His sullen tone was irritating her. "Am I bothering you, Samuel?" she finally snapped. "Because I can take my irritating presence elsewhere if you'd like."

Sam sighed. "No, I'm sorry. I feel like hell. My mom refuses to leave me alone, and Jane keeps calling to check on me."

"Wow, poor guy. I'm sorry you have so many people who care about you."

Sam made a sound in his throat that resembled what one would expect from a cantankerous bear. Charlotte laughed. She couldn't help it. Then she couldn't stop. Tears flowed down her cheeks, and she wrapped her arms around her belly, tipping sideways on the couch. Sam's face melted into a look that was more of a grimace than a smile. "Don't make me laugh," he choked out, "you don't know how much it hurts to laugh."

Charlotte mopped at her face with her shirt, then accidentally released a hiccupping snort. Sam barked a laugh that melded into a gasp. "Ass-hole," he groaned, pressing a hand against his side.

"I'm sorry," Charlotte wheezed. In a wild swing of emotion, the tears in her eyes were suddenly no longer from amusement.

Sam, of course, noticed the shift. "Chuck, what's wrong?"

"Oh, I just… I don't know what I would have done if something had happened to you." Letting the words, the fears, past her lips made them real, albeit belated. She put her face into her hands and tipped forward on herself, ashamed, relieved. "Oh God, you must think I'm such an idiot." Sobs wracked her as she fought for composure.

The couch creaked under his labored movements. "Chuck, come here. I can hardly move."

Charlotte turned, going up on her knees beside him and cautiously putting her arms around him. He leaned into her, pressing his face into the crook of her neck. Charlotte held him tight as she dared, letting her tears fall silently into the sun-bleached strands of his hair.

"It scared me too, Chuck," he said after a moment, his words warm on her skin. "I haven't slept well since it happened."

"Ever since I got that phone call, all I can think about was how close we were when we were kids. About how much I miss you being a regular fixture in my life."

A shudder ran through Sam's shoulders.

"I realized something in that waiting room." Charlotte's breath hitched, and she squeezed Sam a bit tighter, though not as tight as she wished. She needed to feel the solidness of him. The aliveness. "You're my best friend, Sam Stevenson."

It was his breathing that jerked this time, warm over her skin. Cautiously, Sam raised his hand and pressed it into her curls. They sat that way for a long time until Charlotte's knees complained and Sam's breathing labored from twisting to the side. They sat there until Alice came in with a dish of cookies and stood uncertainly while they eased away from each other, wiping their cheeks. Alice's eyes were wet and jewel-bright. Uncharacteristically, she set down the plate and left the room without a word.

L.E. WAGENSVELD

# CHAPTER 20

"Hey, you."

The cheer in Jane's voice made Sam's teeth ache. The encounter with Charlotte had drained him. The woman had a way of taking it out of him sometimes, but in a way that left him slightly dazed. A sensation not unlike being buzzed on alcohol. He smiled at the memory of her laughter, how hard it had been not to join her. Then the smile melted, and he swiped to answer the call.

"Hey," he said finally, remembering you answered when someone greeted you.

"How's my favourite patient?" Jane sounded tired but cheerful.

"I'm fine. Some pain, itching with the laceration on my face. All the norm. And technically, I'm not your patient."

Silence. Sam winced. God, he was such an asshole. What was wrong with him?

"How are you, Jane?" he asked after a few beats of silence.

Jane's sigh echoed through the line. "I'm all right. Long shift. I stayed up to try to get a hold of you."

Sam winced. The motion tugged the stitches and renewed the itching on his face. He tried to muster the energy to feel guilty for neglecting Jane. She'd been good to him, and he was treating her like shit.

"Sorry," he said. "Chuck was here, and my mother hasn't given me a second of peace. I haven't had a chance to call, but I should have."

"Chuck." Her voice prolonged the name in a tone broaching on annoyance. "I didn't realize until you were admitted at the hospital that the Chuck you always talk about is a woman."

"I hardly think I always talk about her," Sam said, more sharply than he intended.

Jane paused, then said, "So, is she your cousin or something?"

"No, my friend. I've known her since we were kids."

"She's quite the loud little thing, isn't she? Reminded me a bit of those troll dolls... Just because of the hair!" she added with haste. "She has so much of it." Jane released a laugh at her own joke, and Sam had to clench his hand against the urge to hang up on her.

"Jane." Her name came out sharp, and he struggled to tamper his tone. "It's time for my pain meds, and we both need to sleep. Can I talk to you tomorrow?"

"Of course, I—"

"Night." Sam disconnected before she finished speaking and banged his cell against his forehead a few times. "Dad!" he bellowed finally. "Will you give me a hand?"

Dan appeared in the doorway, both hands raised.

"If you clap again," Sam said, "I swear to God, I'll find another junkie to finish the job."

Dan scowled. "Don't let your mother hear you talk like that."

"She's already trying to put me into a diabetic coma." Sam waved a hand at the coffee table. Alice had pulled it within reach, and it was littered with teacups, cookies, and the odd chunk of coffee cake. "I even made Chuck take some home."

"Just remember, as crazy as she's driving you, I'm the

one who has been with her upstairs all day," Dan said, eyes unfocusing for a moment in memory.

Sam groaned. "Is the house spotless?"

"You better believe it." Dan grasped Sam's hand and helped lever him upward. Getting off the sunken old couch was the biggest struggle. Once he was on his feet, he'd be fine.

"Did she take a toothbrush to the tile grout yet?"

"No," Dan said. "Made me do it."

Sam rubbed a hand across the back of his neck. "I'm sorry, Dad."

"And the toilet bowls," Dan added.

Sam took a tentative step forward. "I scared her pretty bad, huh?"

Dan's hand left Sam's shoulder but hung close. His father watched closely as he walked, ready in case Sam stumbled. Sam almost didn't hear him when he said, "You scared all of us, son."

L.E. WAGENSVELD

# CHAPTER 21

They were sitting so close together on the old floral-patterned couch in the Stevensons' basement that Charlotte's thigh was pressed against Sam's. Charlotte couldn't keep her thoughts on the movie. Not with the heat seeping through his plaid pajama pants and into her jean-clad skin.

She shifted, enjoying the way his long body tipped ever so slightly into hers when the old springs gave under her weight. He sat with one arm wrapped around his ribs. The way he sat most often since he'd been hurt, and his fingers were only inches away from hers. Every few seconds, she considered reaching out and brushing against them to see what he would do.

Something happened on the screen. Dan jumped, and a ripple of laughter moved through the group. Like the clueless kid who didn't get the punchline, Charlotte joined too late, and Sam noticed.

A ripple of pain warped his features as he turned to her, tipping his lips to her ear. "Everything all right?" His warm breath tickled across her cheek, and she couldn't quell the shiver that ran through her.

"Yeah, I'm good." Charlotte forced her mouth into a

smile. Her gaze wanted to drop and trace the curved edges of Sam's lips, but she convinced it that it would be more prudent to stay on his face.

Good grief, when had she turned into such a sex-obsessed maniac? Her inner voice reared its head to answer. Charlotte liked to picture a frowning middle-aged woman, cigarette dangling from red-caked lips, who spat vowels like a machine gun. *Cuz ya ain't gotten laid in six months, Baker. Cobwebs are forming on your bits.*

"Shut up," Charlotte muttered, settling further into the couch's embrace.

"Sorry?" Sam glanced at her in surprise.

"Not you," she mumbled, blood surging up her neck.

Sam scowled and shifted his gaze from side to side, a smile playing at the corners of his lips. "Okay then."

The basement door chose that moment to bang loudly open, spitting out someone who tripped over a cushion and swore in the near dark. Alice squeaked in surprise and grabbed Dan's arm.

"Ack! Why is it so dark down here?" Sawyer recovered his balance and flicked on the lights, eliciting a round of protests from his gathered family. "Hey, are you guys watching a movie without me? What the hell?"

Dan growled and threw a pillow at his son's head. Sawyer caught it and grinned. Then his gaze fell on Charlotte, curled up beside Sam, and his blond brows inched higher.

"Oh, man! Is this a double date?" Grinning his signature grin, Sawyer stepped behind the couch and put his arms around both their shoulders. "It's about time."

Charlotte's face flamed again.

"Shut up." Sam took a feeble swing at his little brother, then yelped in pain.

"What are you watching?" Sawyer circled the couch and plopped down in front of them on the floor, using his pilfered pillow as a seat.

"*Psycho,*" Dan muttered. The inflection in his tone

implied the title was more for his son, less for the movie.

"I see what you did here." Sawyer looked over his shoulder at Sam and winked. "The ol' scary movie bit."

"Nobody did anything," Sam growled.

"Believable, that *is* your standard modus operandi."

"Don't pretend you know any Latin," Sam snapped. "You'd had to have graduated for that."

"Sam!" Alice popped up from where she reclined against Dan's chest, methodically stuffing popcorn into her mouth. "Sawyer's just teasing you because he missed you. And he graduated." A mischievous smile crossed her face, and she added, "*Barely*."

Sawyer chuckled, ignoring her dig, "No, Ma, I'm teasing him because he's chickenshit."

Sam growled and knocked a knee against Sawyer's back. "You're an idiot. Why are you here? Carmen sick of you already?"

"Boys." Alice had not lost the use of her 'mom voice' since her children had grown up, and she brought it out, scowling at both of them.

Sawyer opened his mouth, but Dan's frustrated roar drowned him out. "Would you two shut up! I'm watching a movie!"

"Better yet, I'll leave." Sam levered off the couch. Pain flared in his eyes, and Charlotte jumped up, hands raised to help him. He brushed her away and stepped around his brother with a grunt. "I don't need any goddamn help."

Sawyer jumped to his feet, "Sam, come on, man." He tried to hook his brother's arm, but Sam jerked away. Sympathy at what the movement must have cost him flared in Charlotte's chest.

"You're all only here because you feel sorry for me. Well." Sam's scowl fell on Sawyer. "Except you, I'm not clear on why you're here. I don't need your pity. I am fine. Chuck, it's Saturday night, and we aren't teens. Shouldn't you have a date or something?" He didn't look at her as he seized the railing and started his painful way up the stairs.

Anger and hurt prickled through Charlotte. She jumped to her feet, planting herself in front of Sawyer when he moved to follow his brother. "What is wrong with you! When are you going to learn to shut the hell up?" she demanded.

Sawyer had the good grace to flush. "I didn't think—"

"Of course, you didn't. That's a habit of yours, isn't it?"

From his corner of the couch, Dan slow clapped. Charlotte glared at him. She had had about enough of the Stevenson men for one night. The entire cantankerous, ridiculous lot. Alice stared at her. Mortification was painted on her sweet face in bright red. Charlotte met her gaze for a moment, sighed, and then turned to follow Sam.

# CHAPTER 22

Sam's embarrassment only heightened his frustration. He knew better than to let Sawyer's teasing get to him, and yet, he let it happen time and time again. Being here at his parents, watching Chuck grow pink and flustered when Sawyer entered the room. It was as if he had reverted to his painful, awkward teen years. All the old insecurities as he watched his little brother grow more confident, more charming. Interested in all the things their father had wanted Sam to be involved in. Puberty had waved a magic wand over Sawyer the instant it hit while Sam sat back, quiet and skinny as his braces cranked his teeth straight.

He was an idiot. Easing down onto the bed, he wrapped both arms around his ribs and tried to find a position that didn't cause pain to echo through his body.

"Sam?" A light rap sounded on the door.

Sam closed his eyes. *Go away, Chuck.*

"Sam?" The knob turned. Childhood rooms rarely had doors that locked.

"Hey, I'm… I'm not dressed." He winced at the lie. "I just want to get some sleep."

A long pause, so long he thought she had walked away. And then, "Do you need help? You're supposed to be careful."

"I'm fine. Jane wrapped them at my appointment today. I won't put a shirt on."

The thought of Chuck's fingers moving over his skin, adjusting wraps, and pulling on clothes sent a surge of heat through him, further scattering his ricocheting thoughts. Why the hell had he mentioned Jane? Sam longed to get up and go to the door. He wanted to pull it open and take Charlotte in his arms, breathe in the sweet scent of her until he drowned in it.

Then her voice came through the thin wood panel. "Oh, okay. Goodnight then."

Sam was irrationally sure he sensed Charlotte pull away from the door. Then her steps sounded down the hall, and he knew it was true, and even when they faded, the hurt in her voice stayed with Sam until he drifted into a restless sleep.

\*\*\*

Two missed calls and a text from Jane, four missed calls from Sawyer. Nothing from Charlotte. Sam knew because he ignored the first two and scanned his list twice in case he'd missed something. With a groan, he levered himself up from the bed. He hated sleeping on his back. His spine arched. The skin on his face was tight and itchy from the stitches holding it together as it healed. He felt more irritable than ever.

The phone buzzed again, skittering across the bedside table and making Sam jump. He scowled at it. Sawyer. Again. Sam hit *ignore*. He was too tired to deal with his brother, especially without caffeine first. Instead, Sam opened the text from Jane.

*Hey, Sam. Hope the ribs are feeling all right. Remember to take it easy.*
*Looking forward to seeing you soon. XOXO.*

Sam groaned and put the phone back on the table, face-down, before hobbling to the bathroom.

Dan was at the table, sipping coffee and using one stub-nailed finger to flick through the morning newspaper.

"They're thinking about redoing the main street," he commented without looking up.

"What's wrong with the way it is?" Sam couldn't stop the grunt that escaped him as he eased himself into a chair. Dan watched him from under lowered brows for a moment, then rose and took his mug to the counter. Without asking, he picked up a clean one from the dish rack, surreptitiously dumped the remains of his own in the sink, and then filled them both.

Dan set the mug in front of Sam and went back to his chair. "Thanks. Where's Ma?"

"She's watching Sonny today."

"She usually watches her here," Sam said, frowning.

Dan shrugged. "She asked Noah if they could stay over there today."

"Because of me?" Sam frowned. "They wouldn't have disturbed me." Actually, a visit with his young cousin would have been a pleasant distraction.

"Actually," Dan said, pinning him with a look Sam couldn't read. "I asked her to go there. I'm staying home today."

"Oh," Sam said. "Okay."

"Only one car in the shop. Your brother doesn't need me."

A smartass remark flew to Sam's lips, but he bit it back. It was rare to have a moment of peace like this with his father. He didn't wish to ruin it with the knee-jerk reaction to be an ass about his brother.

They drank their coffee in silence for a few minutes. Dan pulled out a section of the paper and passed it to Sam. Together, they spent a quiet twenty minutes. Sam struggled to pay attention to the words crawling over the flimsy grey paper, but his mind kept wandering back to the last time he had been alone with his father.

"Pop." He pushed the paper away and folded his hands in front of him on the table.

Dan grunted in question, caught his son's eye over his newspaper section, and then did the same, facing him with brows creased.

"Why were you at the hospital last week?" Sam asked.

Dan's frown deepened into confusion. "I was visiting Tom at the new place. It isn't far from the hospital."

"Oh, yeah, I know. I guess I mean, why did you text me?"

Dan's frown melted into an outright scowl. "A father can't meet his son for coffee without reason?"

"No... I mean, of course, it's just... you've never done it before." There was something off in his tone that sounded too damn close to hurt. Sam cleared his throat, trying to chase away the sensation in his throat that caused it.

"I was already in the area," Dan said. "I know you go in early Saturday evenings."

"It's only, well, in eight years..." Sam trailed off, picked up his coffee cup, then set it back down without drinking from it.

"I never realized it was something you'd want me to do," Dan interrupted, his tone broaching on irritated. Sam tried to grasp the right words, the ones he wanted. The ones that made sense when he was planning them out in his head. Sam let go of the mug and held his hands up.

"That's not what I'm getting at," he said hurriedly. "It's just... Don't you think it's bizarre you were there? On that day, of any day in eight years, it was that day?"

Dan's look of irritation fell away to be replaced with one of consideration. One salt and pepper brow arched. "Do you think it was some sort of parental intuition or something?" he asked. "I never thought about that." His tone insinuated that was the last thing he believed happened.

"I dunno, Pop, have you ever felt something like that toward me?" He'd meant it as a joke, but Dan's brows plummeted back into a scowl.

"What the hell is that supposed to mean?" Dan barked.

Sam hitched a shoulder against the rush of sadness pooling in his chest. "Only we've never shared much of a connection, you and I," he said quietly. It was the first time he'd acknowledged that feeling out loud.

Dan sat silent for so long Sam entertained the idea of going back to his room. Sighing, he placed his hands on the table and braced himself for the pain standing would bring.

"I haven't been easy on you." Dan's voice stopped him. It was thick with regret.

Sam paused, then eased back into the chair. "Dad, I didn't mean— It's fine. We don't need to talk about it."

Dan held up a broad palm, stopping Sam's words. "No, let me talk. I've left many things unsaid for too long with you."

"You don't have to—" Sam started again.

"Shut up," Dan said.

"Yes, sir."

"See, that's the difference between you and your brother. He would never have listened. He'd goad and pick at me 'til I cracked. Just like your mother does." Dan sighed, aging before Sam's eyes. "Instead, you just leave it be, and we are both so shitty at sharing our feelings that stuff never gets said out loud."

Sam settled back into his chair, wrapping his hands around his mug, more for comfort than the need for more coffee. Dan didn't look at him.

"Sawyer, that ass is so much like your mother in so many ways, I always understood how to deal with him. Sasha, well, she's my little girl, doesn't matter if she's grumpy and outspoken." Dan's moustache quirked in one corner before pulling back around his lips in a semblance of a smile.

"And you, poor kid, were my first, and I didn't know what the hell to do with you. Alice and I were so young when you came along. You were quiet and so damned sensitive, I did the only thing I knew how to do. I treated you the way your grandfather treated me. I thought I had to toughen you up. I thought that was my job." For the first time, Dan met Sam's eyes. "By the time I understood I was wrong in the way I was handling things, I didn't know how to make it right. I'd forced you to hide all those emotions away." He released a long, pent-up breath. "I didn't do right by you, Sammy," he said, his voice gruff and soft.

Sam let out a creak of humorless laughter. Words failed him, and his heart had taken up a thumping in his chest. He blinked hard, hoping Dan wouldn't notice before it occurred to him that was precisely what his father was talking about.

"I don't know why I was there that day," Dan went on. "I don't know if it was fate or just dumb luck, but seeing you there, broken and bleeding—" Dan's voice cracked, and he cleared it with a wet, tearing sound. His hands, the scarred knuckles popping up like chicken bones, flexed against the tabletop. Sam stared at them, struck by a memory of being young and thinking about just how large those hands were.

Sam sucked in a shaky breath and looked down at his own hands while his father continued.

"That was the scariest, most fucked-up moment of my life. All I could picture was you when you were small, crying because you'd seen the cat get hit on the road."

Sam squeezed his eyes shut. He had been six and still remembered it clear as day. Dan's voice forged on. Sam couldn't bring himself to look across the table.

"I patted you on the head and told you life wasn't fair, and things happened. To stop crying about it. I never told you, but I went out that night and buried the cat. Washed the blood off the road so you wouldn't see it when you went to school the next day."

"Why didn't you tell me that?" Sam asked. It would have made the pain of that incident less to see that side of his father. To be given a chance to say goodbye to their pet.

"I suppose it scared me. Scared of the emotion. Your mom was crying, and you were crying, and I felt... I felt as though I'd failed you both somehow."

"There was nothing you could have done. You were right. Life happens."

"You were six. You needed more."

"Yes." There was no point in lying. "I did."

"Part of me always wondered if that was the moment." Dan avoided Sam's eyes. He stared down so hard at the chunk of newspaper that Sam wouldn't have been shocked to see it burst into flame. "I wondered if that was the pivotal moment where I fucked everything up between us."

"Dad—" Sam started. He made a move to reach for his father's hand, hesitated, then withdrew. Why couldn't he bridge that gap? Damn it. Dan went on as if he hadn't noticed Sam's dilemma.

"When I walked into that waiting room, and there you were, my son, your blood all over the floor, I thought my heart would stop in my chest. I didn't even realize I'd moved, and I had this guy's throat in my hands." Dan scrubbed a palm over his face. Sam heard the rasp of whiskers against the rough skin and, in a moment of clarity, saw the moment for what it was. A confession. A cleansing that had been a lifetime in coming. And it was as much for Dan as it was for him. He held his silence.

"I would have killed him, Sam." Dan looked up, straight into Sam's eyes. "I wanted to kill him. Then I noticed the little blond kid sitting there, staring up at us with tears streaming down his grubby little face, and it could have been you. That day the cat died. I had to do better than I'd done for you. Had to give that kid something to hold on to instead of crushing him further."

"Dad—" Sam's voice broke, and he pushed both hands into his face, relishing the pain of pulling stitches as he struggled to keep himself in check. "I never doubted you... you loved me, if that's what you think." His breathing hitched and sent a shock of pain through his ribs.

Dan shook his head. "It shouldn't have taken me thirty-three years to talk to you like this, Samuel."

Sam barked out a shaky laugh. "Pop, I'm thirty-four."

"Well, shit!" Dan threw his hands up. "See what I mean?" A chuckle rumbled in his chest. Shaking his head, he rose and came around the table, squeezing Sam's shoulders before picking up both their coffee mugs.

"I've got more to talk to you about." He dumped the cold dredges into the sink and filled both, adding cream to Sam's. "I hope you'll keep everything else I've just said in mind before you bite my head off." Plunking the steaming mugs down, he took his seat.

"Damn, this sounds ominous." Sam wiped his eyes against his sleeve and squinted at his father.

"You'll be all right." The well-loved chair groaned as Dan settled his weight. "We need to talk about Charlotte," he said, with no more preamble.

Sam's stomach knotted. "Why?"

"Because I'm sick of being patient when it comes to you two. You're both idiots."

"I'm so relieved we've gotten past the whole loving-father thing. Phew." Sam dashed a hand across his brow. Dan rewarded him with a familiar scowl.

"That girl is in love with you, and you've been mooning over her for half your life." Dan released a soul-deep sigh of frustration. "So, what's your excuse this time?"

"I really don't feel like it's your business." Sam crossed his arms—carefully—across his chest.

"Hmm." Dan tapped a finger against his chin. "My son and the girl I've treated like one of my own children since she was a toddler. No, not my business at all."

"Chuck doesn't have feelings for me. Your love radar is off."

The look on Dan's face reiterated the fact he believed his son was simple-minded.

"She had a crush on Sawyer," Sam spat the words out

like an unpleasant taste. "And we talked about us and decided it wouldn't work. We are too different."

"*Had* and *crush*. You didn't see Chuck in that emergency room. How she sat at your bedside. Sawyer may as well have been a cricket for all the attention she paid him."

"If he were a cricket, she would have paid him quite a lot of attention, actually," Sam grumbled. "Chuck hates bugs."

"Samuel." Dan slammed a palm onto the table. "You also didn't see her give your brother shit last night for upsetting you. She turned that Latino temper right on him."

Sam paused, "Really?"

"Yes!" Dan smacked his open palm against the table. Sam's full mug sloshed a tide of coffee over the rim. "I'm getting tired of waiting. Do you think I'm going to last forever? Isn't what happened to Tom evidence that you two need to suck it up and give us some grandbabies?"

Sam's head swum. Charlotte. If he gave her the power, she could crush his heart. They'd tried. It hadn't worked. They had tried... hadn't they? There had been so much turmoil in the time since he and Charlotte had woken up in his bed. "I don't know—"

"Bullshit. You know. I know. Your mom knows. Carmen knows. Your siblings know. Take your pride and stick it up your ass. That girl is meant to be my daughter-in-law. Always has been. You want to talk about people being too different from each other? What about your mother and I? Do we strike you as the 'same' person?"

Sam had no argument for that. Dan and Alice Stevenson were as opposite as night and day, but the fact that they loved each other was evident, sometimes disgustingly so. "What about Jane?" he asked.

Dan flapped a dismissive hand. "Nice girl. She's young. She should concentrate on her career for a while."

"What if you're wrong?" Sam whispered.

"What if I'm right?" Dan countered. "If it's real, then it's worth taking the chance."

Like them, his parents. They had risked a lot to nourish their love. Hurt family and friends. Those wounds had healed, and they'd lived a life full of love for thirty-five years and counting.

"Is it normal to be this fucking terrified?" Sam cushioned the words with a wry laugh, but he knew his vulnerability shone through like a beacon despite the effort.

His father nodded, sympathy flashing in his blue eyes.

Sam reached out to the discarded section of the paper and tapped an ad with his finger. "I think I may have an idea. But I'm going to need everybody's help."

"Thank God," Dan said.

# CHAPTER 23

"You want me to go to a baking class with you?" Charlotte frowned at Carmen, resisting the urge to reach out and feel her forehead. "Together? You and me? On Valentine's Day?"

Carmen nodded, her eyes bright with excitement. "Yes! I know you're already the baking queen, but you've always said you want to practice making those fancy little cupcakes and stuff for when you open your shop."

"*If.*"

"*When.*" Carmen loomed over Charlotte, scowling. Why was she so damn tall? "When," Carmen growled.

Charlotte sighed and folded her arms across her chest. "Fine. Not like I had plans, anyway."

"Thanks." Carmen grinned in triumph and slung an arm around Charlotte's shoulder. "I'm feeling the love, by the way."

Charlotte studied her friend from the corner of her eyes. "Speaking of love. Don't you have a new husband to spend Valentine's Day with?"

Carmen waved a dismissive hand. "We'll hang out later after the class. It's fine. I already talked to him."

Charlotte raised a brow, but Carmen avoided her eyes

and threw back the rest of her coffee in a long drag before wiping her mouth on the back of her hand. "All right, gotta run," she said. She gave Charlotte a quick hug, then breezed out of the café. Charlotte scowled at her friend's retreating back.

"Well, that was weird," she said, turning to Harper.

Harper shrugged, not taking off the cutlery she was drying. "Maybe they are fighting?"

"Hmm... maybe," Charlotte said. The bell signaling an order rang through the restaurant, and she shook her head, going to retrieve it. "Curiouser and curiouser," she muttered, scooping up the hot plates.

\*\*\*

A high-pitched buzz announced Carmen's arrival on Charlotte's front step. Twisting her hair into a bun while keeping up a stream of grumpy mutterings, Charlotte stabbed a clip into the mess and checked her watch. Carmen was ten minutes early. Tugging a few curls free, she slapped on some mascara, then glanced at the mirror and shrugged. "Good enough." She'd cover herself in flour in no time, anyway.

The buzzer sounded again, long and persistent. Charlotte cursed and punched the button. "Keep your panties on. I'm coming!"

Carmen's peal of laughter came tinny and distant over the speaker. When Charlotte got to the bottom of the stairs, Carmen was pacing by the door, little more than her reddened nose sticking out from between her toque and the scarf she wore wrapped around her face.

Charlotte tucked her hands into her sleeves and shivered at the slap of grey, wet February air. "Why on earth didn't you wait in the car where it's warm?"

"I needed to breathe and move around. Also, your crotchety old neighbor was definitely standing beside me when you yelled about my panties."

Charlotte groaned and smacked the heel of her hand against her forehead. "Great. I'll be the victim of yet more hallway glowering."

Carmen laughed, "He really does not like you."

"He really does not."

Carmen was quiet as she drove. Charlotte exhausted her supply of work gossip and all the other mundane topics she could brew up, but Carmen didn't take the bait. It was unusual for the two of them to sit in silence. Charlotte studied her surreptitiously. Was she pale? Carmen's freckle-adorned skin was close to translucent on a good day. In the middle of winter, who could tell? Even Charlotte felt pale at this time of year.

"You and Sawyer are doing all right?" she asked once the silence started to weigh on her.

"We're great. He's hanging out with Noah and Sonny for a little while tonight."

Charlotte could tell by the smile that bloomed across Carmen's face at the sound of her husband's name she was telling the truth.

"Did he tell you I yelled at him?" she asked.

A smile flashed across Carmen's face, and she took her hands off the wheel to give them a single clap as she laughed. "Yeah. He told me."

"He wasn't mad at me?"

"Nah." Carmen bounced her shoulders. "He said it wasn't the first time you've torn him a new one, and he doubted it would be the last."

Charlotte nodded. "Probably not."

"Sawyer is sort of like one of those big, goofy dogs. Sometimes he knocks shit over with his tail, but you can't stay mad because he's so lovable."

Charlotte burst into laughter at Carmen's description. It was accurate, but she hadn't expected Carmen to compare her husband to a dog.

Carmen hitched her shoulders. "Sam wasn't answering his calls for a while. That got him into a tizzy. He didn't mean to start anything. He's just… Well, he's Sawyer. I love him to death, but he can be a tad clueless occasionally."

"Can't they all?" The image of Sawyer in a tizzy made Charlotte smile. She pictured pacing and excessive hair-pulling. "Sam will be okay. Sawyer may be clueless, but Sam takes things too seriously. Sometimes I don't even get how they are related."

Carmen shrugged. "It's those lovely faces."

"Ah. They are pretty, aren't they?"

Carmen pulled into an empty parking space in front of the tall, glass-fronted college building. Charlotte unbuckled but paused when Carmen remained still, her knuckles white from holding the steering wheel in a death grip.

"What is it?" Charlotte asked. "You look like you're ready to puke."

Carmen made an odd noise in her throat, and for a second, Charlotte thought she would do just that, but Carmen shook her head. "I'm fine," she said. It sounded more like air leaking from a tire than actual words.

Charlotte settled back into the warm embrace of her seat. "Maybe we should go home?" She glanced toward the building just as a familiar form stepped into the pool of light from the streetlamp. Sitting bolt upright in her seat, she squinted. "What the shit. Is that Sam?"

Carmen gave her a sideways look so steeped in guilt it told Charlotte everything she needed to know. "Speak of the devil?" she squeaked, teeth sinking into her bottom lip.

Charlotte grabbed her wrist. "What did you do?" she growled.

"I'm sorry. I had to." Carmen pulled free and held both hands in front of her face. "This has gone on long enough!"

"Is he coming with us? Is Sawyer here? Is this some sort of weird double date where the participants are practically hostages?" Charlotte yelled.

"Actually…" Carmen drew the word out as if the letters clung to her tongue, and she couldn't shake them off.

Charlotte narrowed her eyes. "Don't *actually* me, Carmen

Maclean-Stevenson."

"*Actually*, I really don't feel well. I think I may have eaten something weird. I'm going to go home." Carmen's voice had gone high and squeaky, possibly out of fear.

"You are lying, traitorous bi—"

"I love you too," Carmen interrupted. "And I love my brother-in-law. You guys need to work your crap out once and for all."

Charlotte crossed her arms and sank so far down into the seat she could no longer see across the dash. "I don't wanna," she mumbled.

Carmen unbuckled and leaned over so she was lying across Charlotte. She opened the passenger door, shoving Charlotte toward it with her other arm. "To quote Dan Stevenson," Carmen ground out as she pushed, "get your head out of your ass!"

"Ouch!" Charlotte yelped. "Stop it, get off me, you Amazon!"

"Get out of my car and go make adorable cupcakes with a sexy man, damn it!" Carmen yelled, giving Charlotte one last shove. "I love you!" she called. Then she slammed the door. The sound of the locks clicking echoed ominously in the quiet parking lot.

"Fine!" Charlotte bellowed. She kissed her middle finger and waved it at Carmen as she peeled away.

"Hey, Chuck." Sam's voice came low and hesitant from behind her.

Charlotte drew a deep breath and turned. Sam stood behind her, looking as shy as a schoolboy and downright adorable. Damn the man. Damn him straight to hell and damn her heart for the gleeful skip it did in her chest at the sight of him. Damn him for making her miss him so ferociously that it hurt. "Hey," she said, pushing her hands into her pockets. "I didn't see you there."

Sam's lips tightened in the way that said he was struggling to contain a laugh. "How mad are you right now?" he asked after appraising her for a moment. There was a twinkle in his eye that made her want to slap him and kiss him simultaneously.

"I've basically been abducted," she said.

"So, pretty mad, hey."

Only she wasn't. She *wanted* to be mad, but she was too happy to see him to feel anything but joy.

Sam bit his bottom lip, eyes straying to his boots. He wore a thick plaid jacket and a blue toque pulled low over his brow. Stray curls of blond hair escaped around his ears. Charlotte drew in a shaky breath. "Fine," she said finally. "I'm not mad. Just confused. Why all the tricks?"

"I wasn't too clear on how you were feeling about me at the moment."

"Sam—"

He was holding one hand behind his back, and as Charlotte stepped toward him, he brought it around to the front.

"Oh," Charlotte breathed.

Sam's face, already pink from the cold, now rivaled the color of the roses he handed her.

"They're beautiful, Sam."

"I feel as though a suave man would say something charming like 'not compared to you' or give you a snippet of Shakespeare." He shrugged. "Something along those lines, but I'm afraid you only get me, Sam the Suave-less."

Charlotte laughed, accepting the bouquet and lifting the blooms to her nose. Velvet petals skimmed her lips as she inhaled. "You do not entirely lack suave, Sam Stevenson. No matter what you may think."

"Perhaps there is a sliver of suave buried somewhere beneath the shyness, sarcasm, and self-deprivation." He grinned, displaying the single dimple on his cheek. Charlotte longed to raise up on her toes and kiss him right there.

"Always avoid alliteration," she said instead.

"Oops, Silly Sam Stevenson."

Charlotte giggled. "Your parents never got that memo."

Sam shook his head. "They did not."

"Come on." Charlotte hooked her arm through his and tugged him closer, shivering against his warmth. "Let's go bake some cupcakes."

"I hope you know what you're getting into," Sam said. "I'm terrible at baking."

"No. Actually, I do not know what I am getting into. I was underhandedly tricked and coerced into coming here, remember?"

"Oh yeah. That." Sam's steps faltered. "If you really don't want to—"

"Don't be silly. I'm already planning my domination of the entire class." She tugged him forward with their interlocked arms. "Never fear, Stevenson, I'll allow you to ride my coattails to glory."

\*\*\*

"Do you think we'll win baking class?" Sam whispered, leaning close to Charlotte. She laughed, shivering at the cinnamon and wine-scented warmth of his breath tickling over her neck.

"I don't think there are supposed to be any winners, Samuel," she said. Then she grinned. "But obviously, yeah, we will."

"I think the two of you have done this before," the instructor said. She was a spry, older woman with a thick twist of snow-white hair piled on her head. She stopped at their counter to peek at the cupcakes Charlotte was icing.

Sam laid a hand on his chest and shook his head. "I can honestly tell you I've never made Valentine's cupcakes before," he said, his eyes wide and solemn. Charlotte snorted. When the instructor caught her eyes, the other woman grinned.

"You guys are too cute," she said. "Keep having fun together. That's the key. Never forget how to have fun." She winked at Charlotte before moving on to the following table.

"Told you, we won." Sam beamed at Charlotte, and she felt it right down to her toes. She would have kissed him then if they hadn't been in the middle of a class full of people. Seeing as it was Valentine's Day, and everyone else in the room was a couple, she probably shouldn't have worried about it. Sam's gaze dropped to her lips, the smile slipping from his. Charlotte took a step forward, then caught herself. No, as much as she wanted to revisit kissing Sam Stevenson, she wasn't about to do it in public.

So, to shake them both out of their trance, she tipped her finger into the bowl of cream cheese icing and leaned forward. Sam's pupils dilated as he tracked her movements. She took another step, and his breathing hitched. Then, she couldn't stop the wicked grin that welled up and spread across her face as she reached out and smacked the blob of ice right on Sam's nose.

Sam gasped, his mouth following open in mock offense. "How dare you?" he hissed. Charlotte grabbed for his arm, but he'd already reached past her and snagged the bowl.

"Ahh!" she squealed, giggling helplessly as he came at her. She turned, but Sam caught her around the waist, tugging her back into his chest and dragging his iced finger right down her cheek. Then, so quickly she would have thought it was her imagination if it wasn't for the tingles of heat that shot through her, Sam pressed his lips to her neck before stepping away.

"Gotcha," he said, smirking. Charlotte wiped her heated face on a towel, then turned, jumping slightly when she found twenty pairs of eyes watching them.

# CHAPTER 24

"All right. I'm not sure what saying this out loud will do to my already suffering masculinity, but that was the most fun I've had in ages." Sam turned the ignition in his truck, and they sat, shivering in the blast of cold, stale air while they waited for the engine to warm. Charlotte rubbed her hands together as she blew into them.

"Serving wine and snacks was pure brilliance. Definitely the best time I've had in a classroom." She glanced at Sam out of the corner of her eye and added, "Or on a Valentine's Day."

In the dim light from the streetlights, Charlotte could just make out the sparkle of amusement in his eyes. Shadows lay across his cheeks, giving him a streaked appearance as if she'd painted him entirely in frosting. "It did beat medical exams."

After a moment, he said, "I've never gone out on Valentine's Day. I always work so the others could go out." He turned his head, catching her staring, and Charlotte's heart jolted, then sped with excitement. Fear. Sam could still hold her with a look and employed the skill now.

"What?" The word came out breathy and faint.

Sam smiled and leaned toward her, and Charlotte froze.

She wanted this. That was clear in the bogged-down seconds while she awaited his touch. Her lips parted by their volition.

"You've got frosting on your face." His breath was warm on her cheek, his fingers icy. She gasped when they stroked across the flushed plane of her cheek.

"Oh." Charlotte swallowed, struggling to battle her racing heart into submission. "It's part of my process," she said. "Childish abandon in the kitchen spurs the creative genius, didn't you know?" Her cheek tingled where he'd touched it and refused to stop.

"I did not." Sam still watched her. It was impossible to read him with the shadows obscuring his face with their shifting bars. His chin tipped as he cocked his head, one sky-blue eye catching the light. "Are you all right?" His hand hovered in the air between them.

"I'm great." Charlotte's voice was overly bright. "A tad buzzed, full, fat, and happy, just the way I like to be." She winked at him, but he didn't laugh.

"Do you think you'd like to do something like this again?" he asked. "With me?

Charlotte hesitated, but only for a moment. "Yes. I would. On two conditions."

Sam nodded. "Let's hear them."

"You ask me straight up next time. Don't enlist your poor, sick sister-in-law to help with your mind games. Two, next time we do something you want to do. Deal?"

"Deal." Sam frowned. "Carmen is sick? She was all right when I spoke with her."

"She didn't admit it until we were here. At first, I thought it was all part of the ruse you two had concocted, but she didn't look great. Well, she did because she's Carmen and got every good gene in the pool. But you know what I mean."

Sam chewed on his lips, his brow furrowing as he studied her. "I know you're too critical of yourself."

"Whoa, whoa," Charlotte said, holding up a hand. How

had they gone from Carmen to her? "What does that mean?"

"I notice the little digs you make about your appearance, or whatever, and it makes me sad."

Charlotte made a rude noise. "Hi, Pot, I'm Kettle."

Sam wrinkled his nose at her, ignoring her sarcasm. "I wish you could see yourself the way I see you, Chuck. Recognize how amazing you are."

Charlotte's vision blurred. She turned in her seat to stare out the slowly defrosting windshield. "It's funny, Stevenson. I've thought the same thing regarding you."

Sam winced. "Touché." He drew his hand back, but Charlotte caught it, lacing her fingers through his. Sam stared down at them for the space of a few heartbeats, then squeezed back. "Chuck?"

"Yeah?"

The crooked, boyish curve of his lips was back. Charlotte's heart skipped accordingly.

"I really, really want to hold your hand, but the truck is a standard."

\*\*\*

Sam guided the truck to a stop in front of Charlotte's apartment and cut the engine. By the time Charlotte undid her seat belt and gathered her things, Sam had come around and pulled open her door. She looked up in surprise as he held out a hand, helping her step down from the vehicle.

"Thank you," she said. "I'm not sure a guy has ever done that for me before."

"Then you've never dated a gentleman."

She tipped her head to look up at him. "Is that what we are doing, Sam?" she asked. "Dating?"

He glanced down at his feet, then looked at her through his lowered lashes. "It's what I'm angling for. If you want to, of course."

Nerves and excitement clutched in her chest. There were

so many things Sam still needed to know about her.

He paused, chewing at his lip, "Chuck—"

"Damn it, Stevenson! Just kiss me." She stomped her foot, splattering muddy slush on their legs.

Sam threw back his head, and his laugh echoed through the snow-muted night. "Bossy wench." He pulled her close with a jerk, staring down at her face until the mirth in his eyes faded. With his free hand, he reached behind her, freeing her hair from its knot and arranging it around her shoulders with gentle hands. Charlotte let her eyes drift closed. When the curve of his knuckle came to rest under her chin, she tipped her head up. Anticipation coursed through her, making her blood fizz.

"I only want to apologize," he whispered. "For the way I treated you."

"Mmm." She nodded slightly without opening her eyes. He smelled of red wine and cinnamon frosting. The press of his hard, lean body against hers sent an electric charge through her.

"I was tired and angry, but I should never have lashed out at you the way I did. Can you forgive me for that?"

Charlotte stretched upward and closed the distance between their lips in answer.

Sam's arms tightened around her in surprise, then relaxed. Warm hands traced up along the length of her spine and tangled in her hair. Using a fist full of curls, Sam tilted her head back, opening her up to his kisses. Taking control. At the hot slick of his tongue against hers, Charlotte whimpered.

"Come upstairs." She breathed against his mouth. "Come to bed with me."

Sam groaned, dropping plucking kisses along her jaw. "Christ, I want to." She could feel the truth of that statement pressing against her lower belly, but also the hesitation in him.

"I sense a *but*." Charlotte reached her gloved hands between them, cupping his face.

"But... I can't." Sam squeezed his eyes shut, the muscles in his jaw jumping. "Not yet."

"All right," she whispered. Her stomach twisted with sharp disappointment.

"Believe me when I say I want nothing more, Chuck." He pressed her tighter against him, one hand on her lower back. "I'm dying with wanting you, but I'm obeying doctor's orders. I'm sorry." Sam wrapped her up in his arms again, tight against the weather. Against the world. His lips pressed against her temple, and she leaned into him with a sigh.

"Doctors, do they really know so much?" she asked against the soft flannel of his jacket.

Sam laughed, dropping a kiss on the top of her head. "I think I should listen, as much as I'd rather not. I don't want to re-injure myself, so we have to wait even longer."

"I could make some really decent 'using your head' jokes right now," Charlotte muttered.

His muted laugh ruffled the hair where his cheek rested. "I admire and appreciate your restraint," he said. "However, it does still hurt to laugh. Please cease being funny immediately."

Charlotte tightened her arms around him. The padding wrapped around his ribs made him thicker. How had she forgotten about his injury? She hadn't even asked him how he was feeling.

"Thank you." He leaned back enough to look into her face.

"For what?" she asked.

"Being the person who can make me laugh, even when it hurts."

Charlotte shrugged. "I'm not actually that funny. Your sense of humor is just skewed."

"Probably." His mouth was closer to hers now, hovering, and the warmth of his breath painted her lips in a rainbow of sensations.

"Just because you can't come in doesn't mean we can't make out more, does it?" She asked.

"Definitely not." Sam's gaze darkened, dropping to her lips. He tipped his head and melded his mouth over hers, blotting out everything else.

# CHAPTER 25

Charlotte jumped when the door buzzer released its electric shriek out of nowhere. The sound echoed through her quiet apartment while she sat blinking for a second. She had fallen asleep, the book she was reading propped on her chest with a little string of drool on the cover.

Groggy, she rolled off the couch, went to the intercom, and pressed the button. "Hello?"

"Chuck, it's me." Sam's voice sounded from downstairs. "Can I come up?"

"Of course." Charlotte buzzed him in and frantically ran both hands through the wild mess of her hair. A quick mirror check showed she looked passable if a little mussed.

Sam walked through the door and folded her into a hug. "Thank goodness," he said against her hair. "I was worried you wouldn't be home."

"It's my day off. I told you that." Charlotte hid her smile against his shoulder. "What are you doing here?"

"There's something I have to do, and I'm hoping you'll come with me." Sam laced his fingers through Charlotte's and pulled her across the apartment to the couch.

She pretended to consider as she followed. "Will there be food?" Her grin melted when she noticed the seriousness in Sam's eyes.

"Sweetheart, what is it?" she asked, frowning.

Drawing a deep breath, he pushed both hands through his hair. "I'm going to smuggle a dog into the hospital," he said in a rush.

Charlotte blinked, sinking onto the cushion beside him. "You're going to what now?"

"There's a man, Mr. Edwards. He's in hospice, and he doesn't have much longer. He told me the only thing he regrets is he can't say goodbye to his dog before he... before he's gone."

"Oh." Charlotte pressed her free hand to her mouth. "That's the saddest thing I've ever heard."

Sam bobbed his head. "I've been in touch with his friend who has the dog, but then I got hurt." He sighed and leaned his head against hers. "I'm just thankful it's not too late." The breath he released was shaky as it brushed across the skin of her arms. "Charlotte, I have to do this before it's too late. It has been eating at me. I was supposed to do it weeks ago, then everything happened. It has to be now before it is too late."

Charlotte nodded, turning and pulling him into a hug. "I'll do whatever I can to help you." Taking a moment, she relished the heat of his skin seeping through the strands of her hair, the warm rush of his breath against her cheek. "Sam?"

"Hmm?" He leaned forward so he could look sideways at her without shifting them. Charlotte reached back and pressed her hand against his cheek.

"How are you so wonderful?"

He released a quick, jerky laugh. "It's nothing."

"Risking your job to grant a dying man's wish? That's... I don't even have words to describe that."

"I want to help him," he said. Then he shrugged. "Besides, they won't fire me. At most, I'll get a stern reprimand for propriety's sake."

Charlotte's eyes misted. He'd never understand. Never see himself the way she saw him. She settled for kissing him and allowing every emotion that was roiling inside her to engulf them both.

"Will you stay for a while?" she asked when they broke apart, breathless.

Sam released a grunt of laughter. "Chuck, it's only been twenty-four hours since I turned down your last proposition due to injury." He cupped a hand over her cheek, pressing another kiss to her lips. "I want to, so badly. Maybe you're right, maybe the doctor's—"

Charlotte shook her head, silencing him with her mouth. When she drew back, she brushed the hair off his brow. "No, *you* are right. If you hurt yourself worse, we may have to postpone this even longer. It isn't a risk I'm willing to take."

Sam chewed his lip, nodding gravely. "I suppose that's a valid point."

Carefully, Charlotte snuggled into his side. "I just thought we could talk. What did you do today? What brought you to town? You know there are phones. You didn't have to come here to ask me about Mr. Edwards."

Sam propped his head against hers, where it rested on his shoulder. "Two things, if I called you, I wouldn't have been able to kiss you or see your beautiful face, and I was already in town. I had brunch with my parents."

Charlotte smacked him, careful to avoid any bandaged areas. "That started off being so romantic."

"I know, I'm sorry."

"Wait a minute." Charlotte tipped her head back to look at him out of the corner of her eyes. "Dan brunched?"

Sam snorted. "Oh, Dan loves brunch, don't let him tell you otherwise. He even ordered crepes." He leaned closer and whispered, "And a mimosa."

"Bah!" Charlotte exclaimed. "I'm going to bug him endlessly about this. Seriously, to the end of our days."

She felt Sam smile against the top of her head. "I don't doubt it for a moment, and I can't wait."

"Also," she added, "how dare you guys not invite me to

brunch? You all know how I feel about food."

***

They waited until Sunday evening, when the hospital halls were nearly deserted. Mr. Edwards's friend Henry, back bowed with age and eyes bright with the promise of adventure, met them in the parking lot. At his side, a round, jovial black lab waited, tail thumping against the ground as everyone said their hellos. Charlotte squatted, letting the dog lick her cheeks until she fell back onto the floor, laughing. Sam pulled her up as best he could, planting a quick kiss on her cheek before he led them to the hospital's side entrance closest to the hospice wing and opened the door.

"Come on." He beckoned them in. Henry grinned and took off down the hall at a surprising speed without waiting for Sam, Charlotte, or Rocky, whose long tongue lolled from his smiling face in accommodating happiness.

The walk down the hall seemed to take an eternity, and collectively the three of them attempted to cover the clicking of Rocky's nails with their voices. They reached Mr. Edwards's room, and Sam pushed open the door.

Soft snores merged with the click and whoosh of breathing machines to greet them. Rocky's ears pricked, and his black nose inched skyward.

"Come on, boy." Sam guided the dog to Mr. Edwards's bedside. Without urging, Rocky placed his front paws on the mattress and licked his master's sallow cheeks.

One piercing blue eye opened, fluttering as he struggled to focus. "Rocky?" Mr. Edwards asked in disbelief. "Rocky, old fellow, is that you?"

Mr. Edwards raised his head, taking in Henry, Sam, and Charlotte standing side by side at the foot of the bed. His overly bright gaze met Sam's and, wordlessly, he held out a hand. Sam stepped forward and seized it. The flesh had fallen from the foundation of what had once been a broad and muscular extremity. Enough strength remained to convey his emotion to Sam as he squeezed.

With a whine, Rocky clambered up and reclined himself against Mr. Edward's chest. His doggy features were a study of pure joy as he lounged there, panting.

Sam swallowed hard and risked a glance at Charlotte. Her eyes were on Mr. Edwards, watching as he cuddled the dog against his chest. Fingers as gnarled as tree roots, moved in a steady rhythm over the animal's speckled belly. The muscles in Charlotte's jaw bunched and jumped, and Sam realized she was fighting not to cry.

"I can't thank you enough for this, lad," Mr. Edwards croaked. He placed a gentle kiss on Rocky's shiny head. "This is the one goodbye I never dreamed I'd get to make."

Sam shook his head. "Please, don't thank me. I'm only sorry it took so long for me to get here with him."

Mr. Edwards's head bobbed, and he rested it against Rocky's. "I heard what happened. The whole place was shaken right up because of it." His hand caressed the silky flap of the dog's ear below his chin. "I'll never understand what it is that leads people to make the choices they do."

Sam stood silent a moment, digesting the words and testing his emotions on the matter. Finally, he sighed. "The man who attacked me is sick and needs help. I only hope he gets it for the sake of his son." A flush of guilt swept over him. Mentally, he scratched out a note to call the police station and see what he could find out about the boy. Curiosity and worry weighed on him still, and there was no excuse for not doing so sooner. It had been nearly three weeks now, and denial could not change the fact deep down, there was a part of him harbouring a pocket of burning anger.

"Well, we sure are thankful you're all right." Some spirits had returned to Mr. Edwards's eyes. He winked at Sam, jerking his chin in Charlotte's direction, "I'll bet this pretty little thing is too."

Sam groaned. "I'm sorry, Mr. Edwards, this is Charlotte

Baker. Charlotte helped us get Rocky in here."

Charlotte stepped up beside Sam and held a hand to Mr. Edwards. "Honestly, I did nothing, but I'm so glad to have met you and Rocky." She smiled and looked up at Sam. "And you're right. I'm extremely thankful."

Mr. Edwards took Charlotte's hand, but instead of shaking it, he lifted it to his lips. "Take good care of this one," he whispered. The web of lines around his eyes contracted with his soft smile. "You won't find a man like him every day." He held her gaze until she nodded.

"I know, sir. And I promise."

Blood heated Sam's face. When Charlotte looked at him, he dropped his gaze to the floor, pretending he had not heard.

Rocky let out a grunt, shattering the moment of silence, and settled deeper into the bed. Soulful brown eyes studied his audience, then slid closed with a sigh of contentment.

"Oh, that's my boy. We slept like this since he was a pup. They took him too soon from his mama, you know. He always needed extra love."

Sam suspected Rocky hadn't been the only one. The first time he met Mr. Edwards, he had told Sam the story of how he had adopted Rocky only days after his wife's passing.

"Mr. Edwards, I'm afraid we won't be able to leave him here too long." Sam swallowed against the thickness that refused to release its hold on his throat. "But we will give you a few moments alone." He put his arm around Charlotte and led her toward the door. Henry, who had scarcely said a word since they entered, cleared his throat with a sharp tearing noise.

"I'll be along in a moment," he said without taking his eyes off the pair on the bed.

Sam and Charlotte stepped outside the door and stood together in silence. No words lent themselves to the moment, and so they stood hand in hand, their heads leaned against each other as they waited.

# CHAPTER 26

Charlotte sat on Carmen's couch and studied her across the rim of her coffee cup. "You're all twitchy. What's going on?" she asked.

Carmen bounced her leg, a goofy smile creeping across her face. "Well, remember when I almost puked on you the night I forced you to date, Sam?"

"How would a girl forget a night like that one?"

Carmen pressed both fists up to her chin in excitement. "It turns out it wasn't something I ate," she hissed in a stage whisper.

"Ah shit." Charlotte cocked her head and wiggled her eyebrows. "Did one of the little swimmers stick?"

Carmen tried to scowl but failed and laughed. "Why are you such a creep? But, yes! Yes, one did!" Blinding happiness shone on her face.

Charlotte grinned, hopping to her feet to throw her arms around her friend. "Congratulations babe, jerkiness aside, I am so happy for you."

Carmen released her and started pacing the room. "We haven't told Dan and Alice yet, but I couldn't keep it a secret from you."

"I would have figured it out anyway as soon as you

gained so much as a pound."

"That might never happen if I can't stop vomiting." Carmen wrinkled her nose and settled back on the couch. "We are pretty happy, but I know it scares Sawyer. Some terrible memories are cropping up for him. He tries to hide it from me, but I know." She sighed. "He keeps waking up in a cold sweat and refusing to tell me why."

Charlotte nodded. "Of course, those memories are going to come up, but everything will be all right."

Carmen nodded, but worry chased some joy from her green eyes. She pressed on hand to the flat plane of her stomach, "I'll feel better once I know this little bean is healthy."

"He will be. I know it." Charlotte squeezed her hand. "You guys are meant to be parents. It's definitely written in the stars or some shit." She waved an encompassing arm in the ceiling's direction.

Carmen blinked and shook her head as if she could clear the worry from it like cobwebs. "Speaking of meant to be, how are you and Sam doing?"

"We are doing very good." Charlotte smiled enigmatically, knowing the lack of details would drive Carmen up the wall.

Carmen sat and inched closer on the couch. "Have you two... you know, done it yet?" she whispered.

Charlotte blinked at her with faux innocence. "Done what?"

"Oh, come on! Did you go all the way?"

Charlotte shook her head, settling back into the couch. "Wow, are we in grade school?"

"Chuck, come on!"

Charlotte laughed, "No, snoopy Stevenson, we have not *gone all the way*. Nor have we screwed or boinked. He was on doctor's orders to do no strenuous activities for six weeks after the... incident. And after how long it's been for me, you can bet your ass I'm putting that boy through his paces. Strenuous will be putting it lightly."

Carmen let out a wild laugh, then pressed her hands to her mouth. "My gosh, you are crude," she said. It came out muffled through her fingers.

Charlotte shrugged. "I am what I am."

"Oh, my God!" Carmen held up a hand in exclamation to her thought. "If you guys have babies, our kids will be cousins!"

Charlotte sat bolt upright, her heart jumping into her throat. "That's a bit of a jump, isn't it?"

"Oh, shut it." Carmen reached over and poked Charlotte in the ribs. "You know you love him."

"That isn't always enough, you know. Life isn't a fairy tale."

"It can be, Chuck. Don't be jaded. You guys could get married, and we could start our own little Stevenson clan. Can you imagine if they got Sam's eyes and your dark cur—"

"Carmen!" Charlotte barked. "I don't want kids." Then she winced and rubbed a hand over her face before saying in a calmer voice, "I don't want to have children. Ever."

Carmen frowned, a flush crawling up her neck and into her cheeks. "I guess I thought you're so good with them you would want your own."

Charlotte swallowed against a wave of guilt. Why was she such a bag? Carmen was only happy and wanted to spread the joy around, just like every knocked-up woman had since the beginning of time. "Don't get me wrong," she said, forcing a smile. "I'm going to love your little brats. I expect them to call me Auntie Chuck, not only to screw with people, but because I'm pretty sure it is going to sound like Auntie Fuck." She looked away from Carmen, uncomfortable under her silent scrutiny. "I'm just never having any of my own."

"Charlotte," Carmen said, resorting to her teacher's voice to shut Charlotte up, and pinned her with a stern look. "Why don't you want kids?"

"It's 2020. If I don't want kids, that's my prerogative.

Don't make me sing Brittany to you."

"Can you just be serious for once?" Carmen snapped. She actually sounded annoyed, and Charlotte's temper flared in response.

"Why does it matter so much to you?"

Carmen narrowed her eyes. "Because you're my friend, and I know there's something you're not telling me."

"Well, maybe I don't want to talk about it."

"Well, you should, because if you want to start something with Sam, he needs to know about this."

Carmen's words were like ice water sluicing over Charlotte's head. "He wants kids," she said. It wasn't a question. Charlotte knew he did. He always had. He'd talked about it even when they were kids themselves. How in the hell had she allowed herself to forget about that? How had she been so stupid?

Carmen's cheeks flushed even darker under their mantle of freckles. "Don't mess this up. I can't stand how you two act about each other. It's so... so infuriating." She added a tiny stomp of her foot for emphasis. Charlotte had to restrain the urge to laugh despite the churning pit of anxiety that boiled to life in her stomach.

"Hate to break it to you, Carm, but women don't have to have babies just because they're in love."

Carmen's hand rose to her abdomen, protecting it. Her green eyes sparkled as they filled with tears.

Charlotte flushed with guilt. "I didn't mean it to sound that way."

"You can do whatever you want, Charlotte, as long as it's for a real, tangible reason. Not some preconceived problem you're too stubborn to let your friends and family help you with." Carmen's voice broke. She crossed her arms, glaring at the top of the coffee table until Charlotte cleared her throat, fighting the sudden urge to cry.

"My mom had postpartum," she whispered. The words stuck to her tongue, but she forced them free. "The doctors called it baby blues back then. They told her to rest, spend time with her friends, but the problem was she didn't have friends."

Charlotte paused, swallowing hard. "She only had my dad, and he loved her, but I always got the impression it was in the way a moth loves a flame. Fleeting and fearful of being burned." Charlotte drew a breath, studying the knots of her twined fingers. "He worked all day, every day, to support us. She struggled with her English. One day dad came home from work, and I was with the neighbor. She watched me sometimes so my mom could sleep. The lady had thought nothing of it when my mom asked her to take me and keep me safe until my dad came home."

Charlotte forced herself to look at Carmen. She needed her to see how serious this was. The fear Charlotte carried inside her like a secret, open wound. The truth was, she would love to have children, and having them with Sam would be more wonderful than she could express. But she couldn't. She couldn't take the risk.

"The door was locked when my dad took me back," she said. "In the end, he busted it down. When he got inside, my mom was on the couch. She used pills. He was too late. If he'd just come home an hour earlier for once—" Charlotte stopped the spillage of words and hauled in a lungful of air.

Carmen was staring at her, eyes bright with tears while more tracked down her cheeks unhindered. "Holy shit. Chuck," she whispered. "I had no idea."

"Besides my dad, you are literally, and I mean literally, in the truest sense of the word, are the only person I've ever told."

"Not even—"

"Not even Sam. He knows that she's gone, of course. Maybe not the complete story, but that she killed herself. He would have to. Dan and Alice know, of course. They basically took us in when we moved to town. I didn't know all of it myself until I was twenty."

"Chuck." Carmen leaned forward and caught Charlotte's

hands from where they rested in her lap. She had the look of someone about to deliver the sort of speech Charlotte loved to avoid. "I can see where you are coming from with the kid issue now. I *do*," she said. "Every time I raise a drink to my lips, part of me fears I've got my mother's alcoholic gene."

Charlotte waved her free hand dismissively. "Your brother got that, and I'm pretty sure only one spawn is allowed to get the shit genes."

"Shhh," Carmen said. "Yes, Jake got it, but that's not at all how it works. The point is, I didn't, and your mother's illness does not automatically mean you will suffer the same. If you genuinely don't want children, that is every bit your choice, but you need to make sure that decision is coming from a place of reason and not because fear is dictating you. Things are different now. There is support for new mothers, medications if need be, but—" Her grip on Charlotte's hand tightened. "Most of all, you're not a lonely immigrant, new to Canada. You have an entire family who loves you like crazy."

"You're right." Charlotte glanced down at the floor, dashing her fingertips under her eyes. "I've been scared ever since my dad told me the whole story. He says I'm a lot like she was." She laughed. It came out wet and humourless.

"You need to analyze what you really want, my dear." Carmen gave her a quiet smile. "It's only fair to yourself and our Sam."

Charlotte stuck out her lip. "I have to deal with that too?" She shook her head. "That's too much adulting."

One of Carmen's red-gold brows arched. "All of it," she said sternly.

"You don't understand. I have a cargo hold full of emotional baggage."

"All of it." Carmen tapped her finger on the table in punctuation of each word. "Bottle of wine, a box of tissues, unpack it, woman. Dig deep."

Charlotte released a shaky sigh. "Fine. I'll do it."

"Start right now. Practice is good for you."

Charlotte gasped. "I thought you meant alone!"

"I'm your best friend. That's practically alone with the bonus of not being alone."

"Ugh. Fine. My father had a three-month-old infant and little else. He came here and begged for a job from Dan, who also gave us a place to live."

"The apartment?"

Charlotte nodded. "I spent the first four years of my life up there, listening to the growl and purr of machines, smelling the grease on my dad's hands. Alice practically raised me. Clumped me in with the rest of her brood, and off we'd go. I suppose it never occurred to me to see Sam in that light. He was always a brother to me first. A confidant."

"And now?"

Charlotte sighed. "Ever since that first kiss, everything has changed."

"Changed how?" Carmen pressed.

"I think he's the one, and I know that sounds like the worst cliche, but—" Charlotte fluttered a hand, and Carmen snatched it like a bug from the air.

"You need to tell him," she said.

"But he wants kids."

"That's something you need to discuss with Sam. Stop trying to decide for both of you. You guys are past that now." Carmen sighed. "I may not have known you for as long as everyone else, but you never struck me as someone who let fear control them."

Charlotte exhaled slow and long, whistling slightly like a deflating balloon. "No. No, you're right, Carm. Screw fear."

L.E. WAGENSVELD

# CHAPTER 27

"What did you want to talk to me about?" Sam asked, peeking into the bag of food Charlotte had brought from work. Stretching to grab plates from the cupboard, she started to answer over her shoulder when Sam's phone rang.

"I should grab that."

Charlotte plated the food, smiling at the domestic peace of the simple actions. She could almost forget the nervousness that had knotted her stomach since she left Carmen's. Sam's voice, so rich and sure as he answered the call, flattened as he talked. Quietly, Charlotte gathered their dinner and went into the living room. Sam had sunk onto the edge of the couch, his forehead in his hand.

"Thanks for letting me know, D." He disconnected and let the phone drop onto the coffee table with a *thunk*. His shoulders folded forward as he shoved his hands through his hair.

"What's wrong?" Charlotte asked.

At her voice, he straightened, struggling to pull a regular expression onto his face. After setting the plates down, Charlotte settled on the cushions, cross-legged, facing him.

"That was Deena, my friend at the hospital. She called

to tell me Mr. Edwards passed away an hour ago."

Hot, instant tears filled Charlotte's eyes. She reached out and locked her fingers in Sam's. "I'm sorry."

He nodded, his Adam's apple traversing up and down his throat. A curl of blond hair fell across his brow. She reached to push it back and let her fingers trace the arch of his cheek and along with his jaw.

"Obviously, I knew it was coming, but—" His voice cracked and broke.

"You didn't expect it so soon," she finished for him.

Sam nodded again. "We were just there," he whispered.

Charlotte blinked hard. One moment an old man was overjoyed to see his dog, and a few days later he existed only in memory.

"I think getting to say goodbye to Rocky was the closure he needed to let go." She ran her hands over Sam's cheek again, for the comfort his skin against hers gave them both. "You gave him his last wish, Sam. You gave him happiness, closure so he could find his peace."

Sam's breathing hitched, and he leaned sideways until his face hid in her neck. She felt the heat of a few tears burn a trail along her skin. Charlotte clutched Sam against her and let her tears fall against his hair, wondering if the saline proof of their shared grief would merge somewhere upon her skin. Bond them in some way, more profound than was visible to the eyes.

She held him fiercely and marveled at his capacity for love. Charlotte made no move to soothe or calm him. Content to let him spill his pain, knowing it would pass. Sam couldn't do what he did and hold on to every loss, individual though this one was to him, could he? He would shatter. He must compartmentalize it all, somehow.

Why tell him it was all right when, at this moment, right now, it was not? Sometimes emotions—joy and grief— needed releasing. It was clear Mr. Edwards had been one of the special ones for Sam. Charlotte knew that feeling, unexplainable as it was, that connection that sparked with some people but not others.

They stayed that way for a few moments. Until Sam's breathing smoothed, and he seemed to register the closeness of their bodies. Maybe he heard the pounding of Charlotte's heart because he stilled against her. The shift in the energy between them was so subtle Charlotte didn't sense it right away. Then Sam's lips brushed the underside of her jaw, soft as a whispered question. Charlotte turned her head, answering him with a press of her mouth. Drove the point home with her tongue and frantic hands that clung to the muscles of his shoulders.

Sam flared with matching desperation, bringing Charlotte beneath him in one fluid motion, the weight of his body pressing her into the embrace of the sofa. Heat surged like wildfire through her veins, and she whimpered, letting her knees fall open. Sam settled his hips between them. He still wore his scrubs, and the soft cotton pants did nothing to hide his need. Nothing to disguise how Sam wanted her, and Charlotte's mouth went dry at the knowledge. He pressed down, and her entire body bucked upward to meet him.

"Oh, God." Sam gasped. Pulling his mouth away, he stared down at her for the space of a heartbeat, then kissed her again.

"Your ribs," she got out between kisses. "What about—"

"Fuck my ribs." He arched his hips, a pantomime only. Still, a high-pitched whimper ripped from Charlotte's throat.

Why had it all seemed to matter so much? All the notions they'd had, all the stupid reasons it would be wrong. Why had they meant so much?

All the time they had wasted. Charlotte's throat closed. She consoled herself with the here and now. Kissing Sam harder, she ran her tongue along the underside of his top lip, shivering when he gasped against her mouth. When her hands slid into the elastic waist of his scrubs, Sam flinched, pulling back, his eyes near cobalt with desire. He squeezed his gold lashes shut, then opened them. "Are you positive?" he rasped. "I'm not sure I can handle—"

Charlotte interrupted him mid-sentence, her answer wordless. She slipped her hand further down, pushing the material of his pants down over his hips. Sam let out a sound that could have been mistaken for pain.

"Not here." He caught her roaming fingers, kissing her slow and long until she squirmed beneath him, then he stood. "I haven't waited this long just to make love to you on a couch."

Charlotte blinked at the sudden loss of his weight, then scrambled to her knees, standing up on the couch and bringing them face to face. "Take me to bed, then." She wrapped her arms around his neck. "Now, Stevenson," she whispered, running her lips over his neck. Flinching, Sam kissed her hard.

"I have this romantic image of carrying you up there," he said against her mouth, "But—" He gestured at his torso, and Charlotte winced, scrambling to her feet. Seizing his hand, she pulled him toward the stairs.

When they made it to Sam's bedroom, Charlotte pushed him back against the door frame, relishing the heat of him as she pressed herself tightly against him.

"Bed," Sam growled, pushing her back into the room. When the backs of her knees bumped up against the bed, Sam took a step away. "Let me look at you," he commanded. His hungry gaze roamed over her, and Charlotte felt every glance like a physical touch.

Suddenly nervous, her hands fluttered up, propelled by the urge to cover herself.

"Don't." Sam's voice held a note of command she'd never heard before. She froze. Sam reached out and twisted a single curl around his pointer finger. "Don't," he said again, softer this time. "Never think you have to hide. You're the most beautiful woman in the world to me, Chuck."

Tears rose, obscuring her vision and stealing the sight of him. She blinked furiously and seized the hem of her t-shirt, easing it over her head. Sam's eyes darkened, drinking every inch of skin she exposed for him. She didn't take her eyes from his as she reached behind her and unclasped her bra.

Sam sucked a breath that shuddered and exited as quickly as he'd drawn it. Then, so slowly Charlotte longed to scream, he reached out and ran his fingers across the tops of her breasts, running them around in torturous circles. His hands were a pale gold against the caramel of her skin. Her nipples tightened, aching with the need to be touched and suckled. She was thrumming, urgent with want, and yet Sam took his time, tracing the swell of her hips and the curve of her stomach. She whimpered, struggling to remain still. When he slipped his exploring hand between her thighs and grazed the aching center of her, Charlotte covered his hand with hers, pressing him deeper.

"It's my turn." She ground out, yanking the bottom of his shirt so hard the seams creaked. Sam obliged by ripping the garment over his head and flinging it across the bedroom in one swift motion.

A knot held the ties of his scrub bottoms, and she tugged, the elastic waist catching on his hips. She yanked again until desperate. Chuckling deep in his chest, Sam stepped back and kicked out of them himself.

He grasped at her hands, attempting to slow them, but Charlotte was past patience. She curved her fingers around the length of him. Sam's head went back, exposing the vulnerable length of his throat. With a growl, his self-control imploded at last. Both his hands plunged into her hair, and he seized her mouth with bruising force. Charlotte's knees hit the edge of the bed, and she fell back with a grunt. Sam followed her down, his naked skin burning against her inch for delicious inch.

"Now." Charlotte wrapped her legs around his hips, forcing him between her knees. "I don't want to wait anymore."

With a growl, Sam rose, holding her by the waist. His eyes searched hers for a moment. "Please," Charlotte whimpered, raising her hips, searching.

"You've no idea how often I've dreamt of you begging me," Sam said. Fumbling in the nightstand he grabbed a foil square and held it in front of Charlotte's face. "Tada."

Charlotte made an exasperated sound low in her throat and Sam grinned. She watched as he sat back, tearing the package and rolling it on. When he hesitated, staring down at her, Charlotte wrapped her arms around his neck and yanked him into a deep kiss. Lowering his weight, Sam positioned himself against her body. The hard promise of him made her squirm. "Damn it!" she hissed through her teeth. She seized a handful of his ass, pulling him, and at last, with a moan, Sam sank deep, filling her in one silken thrust.

\*\*\*

Rain drummed against the skylight and ran in twisting pale ribbons over the glass. Clinging to sleep, Charlotte blinked and squeezed her eyes shut again. She was so content she would have been happy never to move again. Sam curled around her back, his long body protecting hers like a shell. The scent of their night together clung to blankets and skin. Charlotte shifted, and her body twinged in pleasantly abused exhaustion. Sam moaned, and the arm around her waist tightened.

She wanted to turn and look at him, touch the rumpled fall of his hair. Run her hand along his cheek. That red-gold stubble would tickle her sensitive palm by this time. But Charlotte lay still, allowing the thoughts of the night to seep in and take hold and become memories. She took out her newfound feelings and all the accompanying emotions and studied them in the grey light of morning. Was she in love with Sam? The answer came blazing to life on the heels of the question. *Yes.*

The knowledge was bittersweet. As amazing as tonight had been, Charlotte had not accomplished her goal of speaking to Sam about children. She'd sworn she would do so before they went a step further, and it would make it easier if he didn't want to proceed in light of how she felt about a family.

"Sam," she whispered.

He made a sleepy noise and snuffled his face into her neck, causing a smile to break free at the same time as tears burned in her eyes.

"Sweetheart?" she said, slightly louder, twisting in his arms until they lay nose to nose. Sam blinked at her, his blue eyes taking a second to focus on her in the dim light. Charlotte didn't miss the confused joy in them at seeing her there.

"What is it?" he murmured.

"I need to talk to you."

Sam nodded. Extracting a hand from the blankets, he pushed the mess of hair off her face. "You wanted to talk to me tonight at dinner. I'm sorry that we got distracted."

"Well, I'm not sorry," Charlotte said, planting a soft kiss on the end of his nose.

Sam grinned. "Good, neither am I."

Charlotte drew a deep breath. "This isn't easy for me," she said, her voice already shaking.

Sam's forehead creased in concern. "What's wrong?"

"There's something about me you should know if we are going to do this," she said. "It may even make you not want to... to do this with me."

Sam shook his head. "Nothing could make me not want this, Chuck. I've waited half my life for this night."

Charlotte placed her palm against his cheek, drinking in the sight of him through a blur of tears. Then she told him about her mother, and Sam wrapped his arms around her as she cried in a way she hadn't, not over her mother, in years.

"I don't want to have children," she blurted when it became clear the sobs would not stop anytime soon. "I just can't take the risk that I'll be as bad as she was, that I might do something so terrible. That I might leave my baby motherless."

"Charlotte," Sam breathed, seized her face in his hands, and turned her face up. She fought him, not wanting him to see her pain or the snotty mess that she was. "Baby, stop. We don't have to talk about this right now."

"Bu—but you want kids," she choked out. "You've always wanted kids, Sam."

"I do," he said, voice hesitant. "But I've also only ever imagined myself having a family with you. No other woman has come close to that for me." He gave her a rueful smile, then kissed her softly. "I don't care if that makes me sound like a creep or not. But it is something I want to do with *you*, Charlotte. You've always been the one I wanted, and if we have to adjust that life to make us both happy, then that's something we will do."

"Oh, Sam. Are you sure, though? How can you know?"

"The same way I knew I wanted to be a nurse, I suppose. I feel it in my gut. I know it's the right path. Our path." Sam ran the backs of his fingers over her cheek, then turned her face up, kissing her again, convincing her through touch and taste that he was telling her the truth. "Besides," he said, drawing away. "There's more than one way to have a family. Look at you and my family. Having children doesn't have to be biological."

Charlotte blinked at him. "I never thought of that. There are lots of ways to have a family, aren't there? Lots of kids that need help."

At that, Sam beamed at her. Seizing her hips, he rolled her on top of him, hugging her against his chest.

# CHAPTER 28

The next few weeks passed in a blur. Charlotte would race to her dad's new place after work and check on him. Spending a couple of hours chatting with him, making sure he had everything he needed. He had hit it off with the nurse that visited every day, and more than once, Charlotte walked in on them drinking tea and laughing at the kitchen table. Once she had put in her obligatory good daughter time, she would hurry to Sam's. If he wasn't home, she would shower before he got there. More often than not, they would shower again after he found her waiting in bed, and they spent an hour or two getting sweaty.

They fell into a rhythm. Sam was on nights, and Charlotte would watch television until her head was bobbing, texting with him on the rare occasions he had a break. She would crawl into his bed and sleep until he slipped in beside her the following day.

Friday night, Charlotte entered Sam's apartment without knocking and set the take-out on the coffee table. Without saying hello, she yelled, "I think my dad has a crush on his nurse!"

Sam's mussed head poked out of the bathroom door. He yawned and blinked at her. "Is that so?" His voice was raspy with sleep, and the sound of it made Charlotte's chest feel tight.

"Yeah, every time I go in there, they are giggling like a couple of grade-schoolers together."

Sam flicked off the bathroom light and crossed toward her, pajama bottoms slung low across his hips. Charlotte studied his bare torso for a minute, cocking her head as if she were in a museum and he was a work of art.

"I think that's adorable," Sam said, stopping in front of her to peer inquisitively into the bag. She heard his stomach growl and pulled her eyes up to his face.

"What's adorable?"

His brows rose. "Umm, your dad. The nurse?"

"Oh, yeah, right?" Charlotte waved a hand in front of her face. "Totally, sickeningly cute." She grew serious for a moment. "It would make me feel better, less guilty, knowing he isn't lonely. It would be a lot harder to enjoy this if I was worried about him all the time."

"And you are enjoying this, aren't you, Charlotte?" Sam's voice took on a silky purr, and she jerked her eyes up to his. His mouth turned up into a mischievous grin. "I couldn't help but notice you seemed to be eyeing me as if I were the last brownie in the pan."

Charlotte snorted. "You know me too well, Stevenson." She ran her gaze over his body, feasting on him. "And yes, I am enjoying this. Very. Very. Much." She punctuated each word by sinking her teeth into her bottom lip. Sam's gaze fell to her mouth, and she didn't miss the evidence of his interest. Pajama bottoms did little to hide it.

"I have a surprise for you." Sam came around the coffee table and pulled her up against his chest.

"I can see that," Charlotte said, waggling her eyebrows. Sam chuckled deep in his throat.

"Not that. I took tonight off. Deena is covering for me."

Charlotte pulled her head back to look into his face, her brows raised in shock. "Sam Stevenson, playing rookie. I never thought I'd see the day."

Sam growled and plucked at her mouth with his lips. "It's because of this Charlotte Baker character. The woman has me tied up in knots. She's a bad influence."

"Mhmm." Charlotte tipped her head, letting his lips travel along the curve of her neck. "Didn't you sleep all day?"

"I'm full of energy," he said against the arch of her shoulder. "It will be hours before I'm ready to sleep."

"Whatever will we do to tire you out?" Charlotte asked, her voice full of feigned innocence.

"I have a few ideas." Sam's mouth had reached the top of the cleavage exposed by her v-neck t-shirt. Charlotte moaned, threading her fingers through his hair. "Maybe I'm sleepy," she joked.

Sam gazed up at her, brow furrowed. "Are you tired? We can sleep if you—"

"Good God, Stevenson, stop being so damned nice and take off my pants."

Sam obliged with a growl. Spinning her around, he bent her over the back of the couch.

"This is what you get for rushing me," he said against her ear. Charlotte shivered, pressing back into him.

"I'd rush you more if I knew it would get me this treatment," Charlotte said. Her words ended in a gasp as Sam wrapped a fist in her hair and pushed into her.

\*\*\*

"Since you aren't working tonight, you can come to dinner at your parents' place with me," Charlotte said, snuggling deeper into the covers against the warmth of Sam's chest. It was well past midnight now, and sleep was tugging at her.

"They didn't invite me to dinner," Sam replied, his tone grumpy.

"Too bad. I suspect that, since you are one of the fruits of their loins, you have a standing invitation."

181

"Good God, if you could never refer to my parents' loins again, I would appreciate it."

Charlotte tapped a finger against her lower lip. "Can I call you their crotch fruit?"

Sam made a gagging noise in response.

"I'll take that as a no. So, are you coming?"

"Is my doofus brother going to be there?" Sam asked.

"Yes, and his lovely, pregnant wife."

That made Sam smile. He was ecstatic at the thought of being an uncle again.

"I thought we could tell them about us. I feel it will be fairly obvious, but your mom will be furious if we don't fill them in."

Sam groaned and buried his face in her curls. "They're going to make a big deal about it," he groused.

"I know." Charlotte wiggled around to face him, reaching across the pillows to smooth the lines wrinkling Sam's brow. He resembled the father he was complaining about so strongly that she wanted to laugh. Perhaps it was a mistake to tell the Stevensons before she and Sam had even discussed where this was going. She didn't see a way around it, though, and there was no hiding something like this from Eagle Eye Alice. More than anything, Charlotte hoped they wouldn't join the list of people with broken hearts if this all went south on her and Sam. She shook the thought away. There was no reason to think this would lead anywhere but happiness.

"It's going to be like a big thing. And Mom is going to cry because that's what she does." Sam let out a pained sigh. "Maybe we should wait a little longer."

Charlotte raised a brow. "Are you ashamed to be with me, Stevenson?"

Sam had the good grace to look genuinely horrified. "No!"

Charlotte chuckled and inched closer across the bed. "So, you'd rather go all night and not touch me?" She pressed her body against his, her hands exploring hidden, blanket-warmed skin in illustration. "Or without kissing me?"

She caught Sam's mouth with hers, sliding her tongue across his in soft strokes until his breathing hitched and his hands floated up to cup her jaw. Sam groaned deep in his throat.

"But," he argued against her mouth. "If we don't tell them, we could have secret trysts." Grinning, he flung the blankets over their heads. "I could sneak away, and you would have to wait five minutes to follow, of course." Pushing his nose against the underside of Charlotte's jaw, he nudged her head to the side. His lips burned a trail of kisses along her neck and down into the dip of her collarbone. A shiver wracked Charlotte's body.

"Mmm, of course." Her hips arched, seeking.

"I'd meet you in the basement. No lights." One large palm settled over Charlotte's eyes, blocking her vision. Instantly, her other senses sharpened every molecule of her, attuned to Sam.

"Then what?" Charlotte whispered.

"I'd lay you down. You'd be wearing a skirt." His breath cooled the skin he had left damp with his kisses.

"What? A skirt? I'm not sure I own one of those." Charlotte turned her lips, seeking his, but Sam held himself just out of reach.

"Hey," he said. "This is my fantasy. Get your own."

"Sorry."

"I'd lay you down," he repeated, pressing his weight into her. "Slide my hands under your skirt." Searching fingers roamed low, finding the backs of her knees and traveling upward. Charlotte rose into the touch, a moan bubbling at her lips. Sam kissed the sound away.

"Shh, we have to be quiet, remember?"

Charlotte nodded, unable to tear her eyes from his face. The blankets had slipped back off his shoulders, letting the lamp light catch his eyes. They were twinkling, and with his hair mussed and the dimple on his cheek, he oozed playfulness. Her heart skipped a few times in rapid succession at the teasing. Her Sam, comfortable and enjoying himself. The emotions he stirred were enough to make her giddy.

"Naturally," he continued, "we must hurry, but lucky for you, I'm a gentleman, and a gentleman always makes sure that his lady is ready." The hand settled between her thighs, one exploring finger slipping across her folds. Charlotte jerked, a sharp gasp tearing from her. She thrust her hips up, demanding. He was ready, but he continued his sweet torture, locating the hard nub that made her writhe against his hand.

"Please," Charlotte whimpered.

"I'm going to occupy your mouth somehow before they hear you." He lowered himself onto one elbow, the sweet weight of him pressing her into the mattress. Capturing her lips, Sam kissed her. He kissed her until her breath came in gasping sobs. His fingers kept a steady rhythm between her thighs, and she clutched the sweat-slicked skin of his back.

"Hurry, before they notice we're gone," she gasped against his mouth. With a throaty groan of consent, he sank down to meet her at last.

\*\*\*

"See, we came in together, and now they are all staring." Sam, his playfulness spent, scowled as they pulled off their shoes in the entryway of the Stevensons' house.

"Sam, we've known each other for eons. I hardly think this is the first time we've entered the house together." Charlotte backhanded him lightly across the chest. "Also, there is the fact that literally, no one has noticed we are here."

It was true. The familiar bantering voices and the clang of pots reached them from the kitchen of the Stevenson family home. The cacophony was accented by the deep rumble of male voices and broken up by a smattering of cheers and swear words from the living room.

"Ahh, humans in their natural, sexist environment." Charlotte stuck her tongue out at Sam, and he gnashed his teeth in a pantomime of snapping it off.

A high-pitched yelp sounded, and a flurry of limbs tumbled out of the playroom and across the hallway runner.

"I had it first!"

Another scream, laden with impending tears, rang in their ears. Throwing Charlotte a wince, Sam wadded into the fray and came up with a kid in each hand.

"What's going on here?" His attempt at being the voice of authority made Charlotte smile.

"Uncle Sam?" Sasha's youngest, Trey, blinked up at his uncle, surprised enough to forget his tears.

"The one and only," Sam said, grinning at the boy.

Sam looked down at Lily in his other hand. "Hey, squirts. What are you fighting about?"

"He won't share anything." Lily rolled her eyes dramatically and slumped against her uncle's side. "Grandma said we had to split the cookie she gave us, and his side was way bigger."

"No, it wasn't! You're lying!"

Sam looked up at Charlotte with wide eyes. Stepping back, she shook her head and held her palms upward, barely controlling her laughter. Scowling, Sam turned back to the kids.

"I've got an idea," he said. "How about stopping your whining and hug your uncle? I haven't seen you guys in a month. If you stop fighting, I'll make sure Grandma gives you both a cookie after dinner."

Sugar feud forgotten at the promise of more, both children dog-piled their uncle. When Sam got to his feet, he put an arm around Charlotte's waist. "Grandma should have been smart enough to cut the cook in half first," he muttered in her ear, shepherding the pair of rug rats ahead of them into the kitchen.

Alice rushed over, kissing Sam and then Charlotte on the

cheek, but she seemed to take no note of the arm Sam held around her waist. When Charlotte glanced at Sam, he looked so close to disappointed she had to clamp a hand over her mouth to keep from laughing.

Carmen looked up, noted said arm, let out a little squeak, and grinned. Charlotte shook her head and slipped away from Sam to join her friend.

"Hey, Jerk." Sasha looked up from the pot she was stirring and narrowed her eyes slightly at her brother.

"Hey, Brat." Grinning, Sam went and brushed a kiss across her cheek before he branched off for the living room.

"So? How're things?" Carmen bumped her shoulder against Charlotte's.

"Things are good," she said, unable to wipe the sloppy grin off her face.

"What's going on?" Alice looked at the two of them, curiosity brightening her already glowing features.

"Tell her," Carmen demanded.

"Well, now you have to." Alice seized the edges of her apron, looking as if she would bounce around the room if she were forced to wait a moment longer for the news. Sasha dried her hands and came over, studying them with a more stoic face than her mother. "Something is going on," she said.

"Sam and I—" It was all that needed to come out of Charlotte's mouth before Alice was across the room and grabbing her in a chokehold of a hug.

"Oh, yes, yes, yes! At last!" She bounced up and down, her hold on Charlotte threatening to rattle her teeth. Tears shone in Alice's eyes when she held Charlotte at arm's length and stared at her, beaming. "I've been waiting so long."

Sasha watched their antics for a moment, one dark brow raised. "Finally, is right," she said before returning to business. Charlotte didn't miss the smile playing at the corners of her mouth or the twinkle in her Stevenson blue eyes.

"Oh, this is the best news!" Alice wrapped her arms around Charlotte and Carmen, squeezing the three of them together.

"Now, you tell her yours." Charlotte gasped, struggling to breathe. "Quick, before we pass out."

"Shouldn't we wait for the guys?" Carmen asked, her cheeks going so pale it made her freckles pop.

"Nah, they can find out soon enough. This is women talk." Charlotte winked at Alice, who had her head cocked, studying Carmen.

"Oh, my God," she breathed. "You are, aren't you?"

Instinctively, Carmen's hand rose to her abdomen. Alice let out a garbled cry and seized her daughter-in-law in another hug. In seconds, the two women were sobbing and attempting to talk simultaneously.

"Oh, good grief." Charlotte went to the fridge, grabbed two beers, and passed one to Sasha. Together, they watched as the pair mopped tears off their cheeks.

After a few minutes, Charlotte sighed and clinked her bottle against Sasha's. "Let me know when you two ninnies finish," she called. "I'm going to go have a beer with the guys."

Sasha sighed and nodded, turning to follow Charlotte out of the room. "Good call, I'll go with you."

L.E. WAGENSVELD

# CHAPTER 29

Charlotte woke up to Sam standing over her, dressed for work.

"Wow, Stevenson." She stared up at him and blinked a few times. "Didn't anyone ever tell you looming over people while they are sleeping is creepy?"

Sam laughed and bent the rest of the way down to press a kiss against her forehead.

"I wasn't looming. You just caught me about to wake you. They called me to work, and I have a favor to ask you."

"No, I won't do it," she yelled, then yanked the blankets over her head.

"I didn't even ask you yet." Sam laughed, trying to yank back the covers back. When he couldn't budge them, he settled for poking her until she used up her air laughing and was forced to emerge.

\*\*\*

"Hello, I'm Charlotte Baker. Sam Stevenson said he'd call and let you know I would take his shift today?"

Charlotte closed the door to the SPCA building, fully engulfing herself in the scent and sounds of the animals.

The girl behind the desk looked up from her files with a friendly, somewhat harried smile. "Hi, Charlotte. Thank you for coming. I'm Naomi. Will you follow me? I'll set you up with some dogs."

Twenty-odd canine faces popped to attention when the two women entered the room. Some grinned and wagged excitedly, pressing at the bars. Others sat back, watching with wary eyes that broke Charlotte's heart.

"I'll give you two dogs to start with," Naomi said as she took a double-clipped leash off a hook. "Sam likes to take four, but he's bigger than us, and I suspect a little crazy."

Charlotte laughed. "You know him well then?"

"Sam's been volunteering here in this branch for years. At Christmas, he donates his entire paycheck to the shelter."

Charlotte blinked, taken aback. "He does?"

The other woman bobbed her head. "We built a dog run out in the back even. It has a plaque with his name on it and everything. He basically paid for the whole thing. What didn't come out of his pocket, he helped us raise with bottle drives and stuff. We dedicated it to him, even though he forbade us from doing so."

Charlotte shook her head. "That sounds like Sam."

"So." Naomi paused outside the cage of a grinning, scruffy fellow who reminded Charlotte of the Benji from her childhood and cast Charlotte a quick sideways glance. "Are you Sam's girlfriend? I never heard him mention anyone, is all. But a guy like that..." she trailed off, her cheeks darkening.

"I am," she said. The words left a warm glow in her chest every time she said them. Charlotte squatted next to the door and extended a hand to the dog. "I've known him since I was little. He and his siblings and I all grew up together, and we just recently started dating."

Naomi nodded. "Those are the best types of relationships, in my opinion." She gestured to the dog with her chin. "This is Tenley. She's a mixed terrier breed," she said, directing the subject away from Sam.

Charlotte greeted the dog, laughing when the little mutt flopped onto her back, nearly knocking Charlotte to the floor with her eagerness for a belly rub.

Naomi selected another cage. "This guy just came in a couple of days ago. His owner passed, and the friend who was taking care of him just wasn't able to commit full time." She slid the latch back and opened the door. "Come on, Rocky, old fella." She patted her knee, and a glossy black body strolled out of the cage. "He's just the sweetest thing."

"Oh, my God!" Charlotte gasped, and she dropped back to her knees, tangling herself in the leashes. "Rocky, honey! It's you." Rocky butted his head against hers, happily slurping at her face. Charlotte looked up, tears blurring her vision. "Sam is going to need this dog," she said before bending to kiss Rocky's head.

Naomi looked confused. "Sam told me he couldn't have a dog of his own."

"Well, that's going to change. Sam has his parents and me, and we are going to give Rocky a home."

Charlotte told her the story of Mr. Edwards and Rocky's adventure through the hospital. By the time she finished, Naomi was staring at the dog with tears in her own eyes.

"Please," Charlotte said, "I know you have procedures and stuff, but can you help me with this? I swear Rocky will be in excellent hands."

Naomi nodded. "I know he will." She drew a shaky breath and squeezed Charlotte's arm, her pretty face splitting into a grin. "I'll start the paperwork while you are out walking."

\*\*\*

Charlotte's hands were shaking on the steering wheel by the time she parked the car in front of Sam's apartment building. She grabbed her phone and hit *call* on Sam's number, taking a deep breath.

"Hello, beautiful." He answered after the second ring, his voice groggy. With a pang, Charlotte realized she had forgotten Sam was sleeping after his shift.

"I'm so sorry I woke you," she said in a rush. "But the craziest thing happened. Can you come outside? I have a surprise for you."

"Mmmhmm," he answered amicably, but Charlotte heard a yawn muffled by the rustle of blankets. "Let me clothe myself, and I'll come right down."

"What's up?" Sam appeared at the apartment's front doors a few minutes later. He had pulled on soft, low-slung pajama pants, and his blond hair stuck out at all angles. Charlotte, for once, found she had no words and just stared at him from where she stood behind her car.

Sam rubbed his eyes, frowning. "Chuck? What's going on?"

Sinking her teeth into her bottom lip, Charlotte stepped out from behind the car, pulling Rocky along with her.

Sam jerked with surprise, then came forward and dropped to his knees in front of the dog, inspecting the droopy, grinning face. "Oh, my God." He gave the dog a quick hug and stared at Charlotte. "It's Rocky!"

She nodded, almost sobbing at the sight of his face. The light caught in his eyes and turned them impossibly blue with excitement and joy.

"He's yours, Sam, or ours rather. I had to put both our names on the registration and swear left and right I'd be helping with him while you are at work."

"How—" Sam swallowed hard. "Thank you," he said, his voice husky. "I can't even believe this." He made to stand, but Charlotte dropped to the ground in front of him. She put an arm around Rocky, raising the other to push the hair off Sam's brow. Words clawed at her throat with the want of freedom. At last, she let them out.

"I love you." They came out hesitant at first, but the look on Sam's face empowered her. She ran her hands over his cheekbones. "I love you, Sam, and Rocky loves you, and I'm going to help you with him, and your parents are too, and we'll make sure he has the best life."

Sam's eyes were bright. He squeezed them shut for a moment, then met hers again. "I love you too." He let out a gasp that could have been a laugh or a sob. "And my knees are killing me." One popped when he stood and held his hands out to her. "I love you too," he repeated, pulling her close. Rocky let out a woof and flopped over at their feet, content to warm his belly in the spring sunshine.

L.E. WAGENSVELD

# CHAPTER 30

"The dinner was wonderful as always, Ma."

Sam leaned back in his chair, reaching out to lace his fingers through Charlotte's. The other hand hung over the edge of his chair, lazily stroking one of Rocky's silky ears. They sat on Dan and Alice's back porch, soaking up the last rays of the day's sun.

"Thank you." Alice grinned, running her hand through Sam's hair once before lowering herself into a chair across from them. Even sitting, she looked ready to spring into action. "I do need one of you boys to help your father move the gazebo before you run out of here today."

"Really?" Dan groaned, "What is wrong with where it is now?"

"The sun isn't coming through the window the way I'd like. I want to sit there in the evenings with my book and enjoy the sunset. Is that all right, Daniel?" Alice raised a blond brow and stared at her husband until his shoulders slumped.

"Fine," Dan grumbled.

"You better let me help you, Dad." Sawyer raised his beer to his lips, casting his brother a sideways look, his lips twitching. "That thing is heavy."

Alice reached over and smacked the flat of her hand against the back of Sawyer's head. Not hard enough to hurt, but he grimaced anyway.

"Listen to the ego on this one." Alice shook her head as if the occasion were the first time she had noticed her son's penchant for cockiness.

Sawyer shrugged his broad shoulders. "I'm not conceited, Ma. It's a fact. I do physical labor, and Sam doesn't."

"So, lifting a two-hundred-pound man for his sponge bath doesn't count as physical labor, now?" Charlotte said, jumping to Sam's defense.

"Chuck," Sam hissed, prodding her with his elbow, "Is that really the best example you could come up with? Just no... please."

Alice moved behind her eldest son and patted his shoulder. "Strength comes in all forms, honey. And anyway—" She bent and added in a faux whisper, "You've got the bigger penis."

Besides Sawyer, Carmen performed an actual spit take, drenching her flabbergasted husband with lemonade. Sawyer gaped at his mother, and Sam made a noise that came out as a mixture between a groan and a sob. Looking at him, Charlotte wondered if a person's head could fill so entirely with blood that they passed out. Sam would probably know the answer but now didn't seem the time to ask.

"Christ, Alice. Why?" Dan threw his hands up, his thick brows nearly obscuring his dark eyes. "You need to learn not to say whatever comes to mind."

Alice batted her eyes in her husband's direction. "Come on, I birthed them, changed their diapers for years. I know their penises nearly as well as I know yours."

Dan rubbed a hand over his face. "Will you never shut up, woman?" he groaned into his palms.

"I haven't after fifty-eight years, so it isn't looking good." Alice caught Charlotte's eyes and grinned. Dan groaned into his hands again.

"Fine! I'm sorry, honey." Alice held her hands up, eyeing Dan until he relaxed and lifted his beer to his lips, taking a healthy swig before she added, "Sam's hung more like you."

It was a good thirty seconds, accented by the pounding of Sawyer's palm against his back before Dan could breathe again. Carmen laughed so hard Charlotte worried the baby may end up oxygen-deprived. Tears rolled off her chin, and she shook in near-silent guffaws, arms wrapped around her slightly protruding middle. Just looking at her made Charlotte laugh harder. Sawyer was rigid in his chair. His face twisted in horror as he swivelled his gaze from his brother to his father, then down to his lap. Finally, he leaned over to Carmen. "You're like... happy with it? Right?" he whispered. Only Charlotte was close enough to hear.

"Oh, God, I can't." Carmen wheezed, stumbling to her feet, with both hands clutching her belly. "I'm going to pee my pants." She rushed toward the house, leaving the rest of the family gasping for breath.

Charlotte wiped her eyes and glanced at Sam, who had sunk as far as possible into the corner of the couch, a frilly, lace-edged cushion held tight over his face.

"Sam?" Charlotte poked him in the thigh.

"Don't interrupt me," he growled from beneath the fabric. "I'm attempting to suffocate myself."

"Please don't do that. I'm in too deep with you." When he didn't answer, Charlotte poked him again. "Sam?"

"Yes, Charlotte?" Sam said, lowering one edge off the pillow to peek at her.

"I want to have babies with you."

She watched the grin spread up from behind the cushion and gather in the corners of his eyes. "Yeah?" he whispered.

"Yeah," Charlotte said around the lump in her throat.

The pillow tumbled to the floor as Sam pulled her into his arms.

*\*\*\**

"Oh, my God!" Charlotte dropped Rocky's leash onto the floor and smacked her hands over her mouth at the sight of Sam.

"It's dinner and flowers and candles." Sam's mouth curved, pushing the single dimple into appearance.

Charlotte narrowed her eyes. "You know what I mean," she said. "You're wearing *it*." She let out a joyous bubble of laughter and walked around Sam, looking him up and down. He wore the leather and tunic she'd discovered all those months ago in the closest. And he looked damn good in the outfit, too. "Look at your ass," she said, running a hand over the body part in question. "Why did guys stop wearing these?"

Sam grinned, and her heart bumped accordingly. "Well, I made a promise once. I thought since you held up your end of the bargain, it was high time I did the same." The deep-green tunic complemented his height and blond hair, and the tan pants hugged him in all the right places. Charlotte could hardly pull her eyes away.

"I'm extremely happy about it." She went to him, stopping a foot away and reaching out her hands. "What's this song?"

"Ed Sheeran, 'Tenerife Sea.' What, do you live in a hole, Baker?"

"Ugh, I know that." Charlotte laughed. "But why are you playing it?"

"Well, someone once told me she thought it was the most romantic song she'd heard."

Charlotte took a step closer to Sam. "Did she?"

Sam nodded. "At Carmen and Sawyer's wedding. I almost kissed you on the dance floor."

"I remember."

"You took Rocky for a long walk. I've had this song on repeat for forty minutes."

Charlotte laughed. "That's a while. Ed has other great songs too, you know."

"It had to be this one," Sam said. "I wanted to see that look in your eyes again."

"It's you who gives me that look, Sam, not the song."

"I know." Sam fiddled with Rocky's ears for a moment, running the silky flaps through his fingers, then took a deep breath and looked her square in the eyes. "Charlotte, I love you."

"I love you too." She reached to touch his cheek, but Sam caught her hand and pressed his lips against her palm instead.

"I've something to say to you," he said, his tone gruff.

"Yes, sir," she replied, biting her lip to contain her smile.

Sam's breath shuddered, and one of his knees popped as he lowered himself to one knee on the ground in front of her.

"Charlotte, I told you once it's always been you. It's you who sees my faults and loves me not despite them but because of them." He scrunched his nose, fighting to keep his voice steady. "There's no one I want to spend the rest of my life with more than the person who knows me best in this world. My best friend."

Charlotte was vaguely aware of the tears dripping off her chin, but she couldn't take her eyes off Sam.

Sam drew in a deep, shaking breath. "Chuck, Charlotte, will you marry me?"

Charlotte stared at him for a drawn-out moment, drinking in the sight of him. Then she dropped to her knees with an incoherent noise and threw her arms around his neck. Sam fell sideways, collapsing them both into a pile. Rocky jumped up, pushing his cold nose into their faces as his tail thumped against the couch.

"Yes," Charlotte managed to say around her joy, Sam's lips, and Rocky's unhelpful snout. "Yes, I'll marry you, Sam."

"Thank goodness." Sam laughed. "I would have really regretted putting this outfit on for you if you'd said no."

L.E. WAGENSVELD

# EPILOGUE

"So, I've had a thought," Sam said as soon as he heard Charlotte open the door. "It may be crazy, and you can feel free to shut me down right now if you hate it, but—" He turned from where he stood at the counter, seeing her hovering in the front doorway for the first time. The color in her cheeks was high, and the messy tendrils of her hair sweat-damp clung to her neck. Sam didn't think there would ever be a day that his heart didn't squeeze with joy at the sight of her. Now, however, he narrowed his eyes. "What are you doing? Why are you being weird?"

Charlotte shrugged, avoiding his gaze. "I'm not being weird. You're being weird."

"Usually, yeah. What's behind your back?"

Charlotte ducked a bit further behind the door frame. Next to her, Rocky sighed, probably losing all hope of ever having his leash taken off, and flopped onto the cool floor just inside the door.

"Charlotte-soon-to-be-Stevenson." Sam took a few strides toward her. "What do you have?"

Charlotte let out a hearty sigh, her features twisting into an extreme look of guilt. Then she took a step inside and another before turning and squatting down. "Come on.

Come on, Tenley." At her heels, a small, shaggy head appeared.

"Chuck, did you steal a dog?"

Charlotte scrunched up her face, shaking her head so hard more hair fell loose from the precarious bun on top of her head. "No," she whispered.

"Did you adopt yet another dog without speaking to me?" Sam struggled to keep the grin off his face. The truth was he'd been thinking for some time of having Tenley join their family, but he wasn't about to let on that she was off the hook just yet. Then to his alarm, Charlotte's face crumpled, and tears filled her eyes.

"Oh, Sam, she's been at the shelter for eight months," she wailed. "How could anyone look at her sweet face and not take her home?"

Alarmed at the sudden onslaught, Sam crossed the room and pulled Charlotte into his arms. "Shhh, I know. I wasn't mad. I'm happy she is here."

"Eight months!" Charlotte went on as if he hadn't spoken, sobbing harder now. Sam could feel the wet warmth soaking through the front of his thin cotton t-shirt. "Eight months of her watching other dogs go home with families while she stayed behind." Behind Charlotte, Tenley let out a worried whine and sat beside Rocky. "It's s-s-so unfair!"

Cautiously, Sam pushed Charlotte back, dipping his head to look into her face. With some struggle, he got her to meet his eyes. "Sweetheart," he said, using his thumbs to wipe the tears from her face. "It's okay. I think it's perfect that she is going to come live with us."

The words he had meant to reassure her only seemed to set her off further, and Charlotte flung herself against his chest, her arms squeezing him so tightly Sam worried for his ribs. After a few moments, her sobs distilled into the odd shivery breath.

"What was your thought?" she finally asked with a sniffle.

Sam frowned. The last ten minutes were giving him emotional whiplash. "Pardon?"

Charlotte stepped back, wiping her nose on her sleeve. "When I came in, you said you'd had a crazy thought."

"Oh, yes." The conversation with Carmen had flown entirely out of his head at the sight of Charlotte. He ran a hand over his jaw, studying her for a second. Did he dare bring it up now? What if she got upset again?

Grimacing, he stepped past her, shut the door, and then bent to unhook the two dogs' leashes. "I was talking to Carm," he said, hooking his fingers through Charlotte's and leading her to the couch.

"Okay," Charlotte said, blinking at him. Her mascara had turned into an ink spill beneath her dark lashes, and he was sure she'd never looked cuter. "And?"

"We had a thought... well, Carmen had a thought that I sort of liked the idea of."

Charlotte frowned, looking more like herself. "Spit it out, Stevenson."

Chuckling, Sam took both her hands and drew a deep breath. "What if we got married during the family camping trip?" He let the words out in a rush, then bit his bottom lip, waiting for her reaction.

For a moment, she looked confused, then dipped her head as if letting the thought roll around. "Jake would be okay with that?"

"Carmen seemed to think so, and nearly all our family would be there already. We'd have to get your dad and Susan to drive up, but otherwise... the gang would all be there."

Jake Maclean, Carmen's younger brother, had offered up the use of his farm a few hours away as a spot for a camping retreat.

"Three months..." Charlotte said, tapping her finger against her chin. "That would work."

Sam frowned. "Are you sure? It doesn't give us a lot of time to plan. I don't want you to do anything that isn't exactly what you want."

"Well, seeing as we don't have much time, I think it's perfect."

A rush of fear spiked in Sam's gut at her words. "What do you mean we don't have much time?"

Charlotte stared at him, her eyes glistening with another wave of tears. "Because, Sam, I'm pretty sure I'm pregnant."

# ACKNOWLEDGEMENTS

Thank you again to my family, and friends who ceaselessly encourage me to continue to write. They read drafts, share posts, and sing praises I'm not sure I always deserve.

L.E. WAGENSVELD

# DON'T MISS THE FIRST BOOK IN
# THE STEVENSON FAMILY STORIES

## BREAKING DOWN

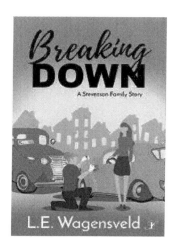

*Get your engine revving with this funny and heartwarming story of one woman's happily ever after with a grease-stained knight.*

Carmen Maclean is unmoored from her home and city when a long-term relationship turns violent. Determined to protect herself, Carmen heads to the small mountain town where her little brother lives, but her plans take a turn for the worse when car trouble leaves her stranded on the side of a lonely mountain highway.

Sawyer Stevenson is a divorced small town mechanic, scared to let himself fall in love again. Lately, he's taken to burying his emotions in ways that border on scandalous. When he is tasked with fixing a Beetle better left to the junkyard, Sawyer is willing to accept the challenge. He didn't count on meeting Carmen, or the feelings she would stir in him.

Carmen and Sawyer can't get enough of each other, despite knowing it won't be long before they have to say goodbye. Nothing matters to Sawyer but keeping Carmen safe when danger follows her to Willow Brook. For the first time in as long as either can remember they are looking forward instead of back, but what exactly does the future hold?

EXCERPT:

A sharp creak of rusty hinges echoed through the garage, making both men jump guiltily as the girl hopped down from the truck. She stretched, then her eyes met Sawyer's, and a crooked smile inched over her face. Gathering up the mess of long, thick cinnamon strands from around her face, she began to twist them together into a braid as she navigated through the maze of machinery toward them. A pair of frayed, cut-off denim shorts displayed long pale legs, and a green cardigan hung around her slim form.

She yawned as she approached, hiding it behind the back of a freckled hand, and Sawyer's heart did an odd little clench within the shelter of his ribs. He pressed the heel of his hand against the spot.

"I can't believe I fell asleep," she said, sheepishly. "I hope I didn't drool in your truck, Dan."

Sawyer's dad waved a hand at her, brushing away her comment. "There's been worse in that truck, I'm sure."

Sawyer glanced at his father; then, before he could think of any comment to needle him with, his gaze strayed back to the woman's face on their own accord. The bruise branded the freckle-dusted arc of her left cheekbone, an ugly mottled patch of bright green and blue spilling like oil across her fair skin. Sawyer curled his fingers into fists at his side. He had to force himself to look away from the mark. Anger, wild and targetless, rolled in his gut. He swallowed, hard. Dan was the first to break the silence.

*AVAILABLE IN EBOOK AND PRINT*
*WHERE BOOKS ARE SOLD*

L.E. WAGENSVELD

# ABOUT THE AUTHOR

L. E. Wagensveld lives in a small town in British Columbia, Canada with her family and works as an Assistant Community Librarian. She loves coffee, is an inexperienced and less than graceful kickboxer, and committed bibliophile.

For as long as she can remember, L. E. has been a passionate wordsmith. From crafting poems about her pets as a child to the various piles of unfinished manuscripts that sit in her magic cloud, she has always found writing a necessity for her life.

Her Stevenson Family novels focus on friendship, family, and love in a small town. L. E is an unashamed romance lover, a passion she attributes to her late maternal grandmother, who was rarely without a Harlequin novel close at hand. With her novels, L. E. seeks to create an escape for her readers, a place to go when they need a smile, and some of those warm, fuzzy feelings.


You can find her on:
www.lewagensveld.com
https://www.instagram.com/l.e.wagensveld
https://www.facebook.com/l.e.wagensveld
https://twitter.com/LWagensveld

.

Manufactured by Amazon.ca
Bolton, ON

32956452R00127